BOOK TWO OF THE PAUL WHITE SERIES

THE MECHANIST

PAUL GORDON
JAMES

atmosphere press

Published by Atmosphere Press

Cover design by Matthew Fielder

Atmospherepress.com

Chapter 1
The Summons

London, August 1892. Summer pressed heavy over London, the heat seeping even into the hallowed halls of the Huxley Building at the Royal College of Science. The grand edifice, standing proudly on Exhibition Road, seemed to absorb the August sun like a monolithic sponge, its Portland stone exterior radiating warmth back into the already stifling air. Built just a decade earlier in 1881, the Huxley Building had quickly established itself as the beating heart of scientific education in South Kensington, its imposing Victorian façade a testament to Britain's commitment to progress and enlightenment.

The building rose four stories high, its large sash windows arranged in symmetrical rows that reflected the disciplined minds working within. Each window was framed by ornate stonework, the decorative lintels and sills softening what might otherwise have been an austere appearance. Above the main entrance, carved into the stone with painstaking precision, were the words "Royal College of Science", letters worn slightly by a decade of London's notorious soot and fog but still proudly proclaiming the building's purpose to all who passed beneath them.

I sat at the back of the lecture hall, feeling myself sink further into my seat as Professor Napier Shaw droned on about meteorology. Ordinarily, I would have tried harder to keep up with the talk, but Shaw's ideas felt almost mystical today, his grand pronouncements about "scientific methods conquering chaos" hovering somewhere between science and prophecy.

He expounded on the future he imagined for his field—a future where scientists could predict the weather days in advance, where even the turbulent skies would bow to order. Determinism, he insisted, was at the core of nature itself. Every gust of wind, every cloud formation—surely all could be charted if we could only account for the variables. But the language felt too lofty, too abstract for my mind to stay anchored to it. Shaw's voice faded into the background, blending with the muffled sounds of footsteps in the corridors beyond.

I let my eyelids droop. In my drifting state, images from my recent work under Professor Dixon flitted through my mind: calculations, codes, a conversation we'd had about logic circuits and the ghost of Babbage's dream machine. The math in my head grew soft and unfocused, then slipped away entirely.

I hadn't quite realised I'd fallen asleep until I felt a firm hand on my shoulder.

"Mr. White?"

My eyes snapped open. I blinked, feeling both dazed and sheepish as I looked up at a young man with an ink-stained coat and tousled ginger-coloured hair. His expression was hard to read, though I detected a hint of irritation in his eyes.

"Professor Goodeve requests your presence. Immediately."

"Now?" I stammered, casting a furtive glance toward Shaw at the front of the hall. He was still speaking passionately, oblivious to my rude awakening.

"Yes," the assistant replied, unimpressed. "Now."

I gathered my things and rose, hoping Shaw hadn't noticed as I slipped out of the lecture hall and followed the assistant down a series of winding corridors. My pulse quickened. I'd had little contact with Thomas Minchin Goodeve, though his reputation at the College was nearly mythical. He was a man whose brilliance was as much a matter of fact as it was of legend, and with it came the stories—of strange requests, of late-night experiments, of assistants who never quite returned the same. Whatever he wanted to discuss, I had a feeling it would be anything but ordinary.

The assistant led me to a modest door and gestured for me to enter. Inside, Goodeve's office was crowded with stacks of books and odd mechanical devices, each one gleaming faintly in the soft, filtered light that slipped through the tall windows. Seated behind a cluttered desk, Goodeve looked up, studying me with the same intensity I'd heard he reserved for his scientific inquiries.

"Ah, Mr. White," he said, gesturing to the chair across from him. "Sit."

I took the seat, feeling the weight of his gaze. I'd been under Dixon's discerning eye often enough, but Goodeve's scrutiny felt somehow different—sharp and probing, as though he were picking apart the layers of my thoughts.

"Tell me," he began, his voice calm but with a subtle edge, "does Professor Dixon currently possess Ada Lovelace's diary?"

The question was so unexpected that I almost forgot myself. I sat up straighter, willing my expression to stay blank as I searched for an appropriate answer. "Professor Dixon... I have no reason to believe that he does, sir."

Goodeve's gaze held mine for a moment longer before his face softened slightly, though his eyes remained just as keen. "Good," he murmured, leaning back in his chair. "And if you're worried about Dixon hearing of this conversation, you needn't be. This inquiry is between us."

I nodded, feeling a pang of relief but also a deepening sense of confusion. Dixon had only ever mentioned Lovelace's diary in passing, hinting at it as more of an elusive curiosity than anything significant. So why would Goodeve, of all people, take such a sudden interest in it?

"Of course, I refer to a copy of the diary," he continued,

almost offhandedly, but the words stopped me cold.

A copy. The implication struck me almost instantly—Goodeve had never had access to the original. And that revelation led to another: if Goodeve didn't have the diary, then it was very possible that Lovelace's widower, William King-Noel, the 1st Earl of Lovelace, still did.

My mind began to race. It was common knowledge that in the year 1886, Lord King-Noel acquired Ben Damph Lodge along with its vast 12,000-acre estate, nestled at the eastern end of Loch Torridon in the rugged wilds of Ross-shire. A retreat befitting a man of his standing, it stood in splendid isolation, surrounded by towering peaks and the untamed beauty of the Highlands—a domain where the echoes of the modern world seemed scarcely able to intrude.

I tried to keep my expression neutral, nodding as Goodeve continued with a few remarks about research and diligence, but my mind was whirring. When he dismissed me, I stood, inclining my head in thanks.

"Thank you, Professor," I managed, keeping my tone as even as possible.

As I left the office and walked through the long corridors, the implications of what I'd just learned grew more vivid. Ada Lovelace's diary, the original—her most intimate thoughts and insights into her work on analytical engines—might still be with her family, untouched, unread by those who might truly understand her vision.

My mind made itself up almost without my consent. On the way back to Nelson House, I paused beside one of the red, hexagonal Penfold post boxes that stood near the edge of the Docklands. I drew out a piece of paper from my pocket, my heart thumping as I hastily wrote:

My Lord King-Noel,

I would be honoured and privileged to engage in a conversation on the matters of science and analytical engines. I believe we might find mutual interest in the groundbreaking work of the late Lady Ada Lovelace.

Please reply to me at my academic address, Huxley Building, South Kensington, Royal College of Science.

Yours faithfully,
Paul White

I read it over quickly, sealing the letter with a touch of finality before slipping it into the post box. There was something thrilling in the act, as though I were slipping a cipher into the flow of history itself, waiting for a response that might draw me further into Lovelace's secrets.

The journey from Kensington to the Docklands was never an easy one. The city stretched interminably between them, a labyrinth of gaslit streets, bustling thoroughfares, and the ever-present crush of hansom cabs and drays. The further east one travelled, the more London seemed to shed its veneer of refinement, giving way to the dense tangle of warehouses, shipyards, and tenements that crowded the river's edge. By the time I arrived at Nelson House, the scent of coal smoke and brine clung to my coat, and the Thames, wide and restless, rolled darkly under the fog.

My mind wandered to this spring's dramatic events. If there is one thing the academic world despises, it is scandal. For a week, the newspapers overflowed with sensational revelations about the late Nathaniel Bullard—a seemingly respectable professor at the Royal College of Science.[1] His academic peers were swift to distance themselves, giving interviews in which they condemned Bullard as an anomaly, wholly incompatible with the principles of British science. They emphasised Dixon's heroic role in bringing Bullard to justice, and

1 We refer the reader to an earlier novel, *The Night's Cipher*, by the same author.

before long, headlines shifted to the Blue Cube's victory over Steinitz, pushing Bullard's name into relative obscurity. His connection to the Whitechapel murders was first mentioned, then disputed, then eventually denied. A few weeks later, the Conservative and Liberal Unionist coalition lost its majority in the House of Commons, ultimately leading to Prime Minister Lord Salisbury's resignation on August 12. These events swiftly buried Bullard's notoriety in the fleeting memory of the public.

For a select few eccentrics, Bullard became a figure of dark fascination. They visited the sites of his crimes in Whitechapel, obsessively sought out any surviving fragments of his writings, pieces of clothing, and, remarkably, someone reportedly paid nearly a thousand pounds for his rapier, cleverly disguised as a walking cane.

I found this morbid obsession deeply unsettling. Humanity, it seems, is irresistibly drawn to the macabre, as if horror provides a welcome distraction from the mundane—or from the quiet, insidious evils lurking in their own lives. For my part, I sought refuge in science, hoping to bury the memories of Bullard's atrocities beneath logic and reason. And for a time, I believed I had succeeded.

As I walked toward the silhouette of Nelson House in Cold Harbour, its form half-lost in the murky fog that clung to the river, I could almost hear Dixon's voice in my mind. Would he approve of my secret quest for Lovelace's diary? Would he sense the same intrigue that I did in Goodeve's slip of the tongue?

These questions trailed after me, mingling with the humid air, as I made my way back to the Docklands and the mysteries that seemed to pulse beneath London's dark, restless surface.

Chapter 2
The Strange Undertakers

As I approached Nelson House, something felt... wrong. A black carriage sat parked in front of the building, its dark shape looming in the thickening evening fog. It was an ominous sight, unmistakably reminiscent of an undertaker's carriage, with its polished wood and grim, veiled windows. The uneasy feeling in my stomach deepened as I noticed two men by the front steps, their shoulders broad and faces obscured by low-brimmed hats. They were carrying a stretcher between them, a body covered with a white blanket.

My heart dropped. Dixon.

I quickened my pace, calling out to them as they reached the edge of the carriage.

"Wait! What's going on here?" I demanded, my voice sharper than I'd intended.

The men paused, exchanging a glance. One of them, a burly fellow with a face weathered like worn leather, turned toward me with an expression that I could only describe as detached—cool, uninterested.

"Nothing to worry about, sir," he said, his voice gravelly. "We're just disposing of the results of a failed scientific experiment."

"A failed experiment?" I repeated, trying to wrap my mind around it. "Who—what happened?"

"Nothing to worry about," the other man echoed, shifting his grip on the stretcher. "No humans have died. Just an experiment gone awry."

The answer was vague, maddeningly so. But before I could ask anything further, the men lifted the stretcher into the carriage, shutting the door with a grim finality. The carriage lurched forward, its black silhouette fading into the mist. I stood there for a moment, staring after it, my mind racing with questions, dread gnawing at the edges of my thoughts.

Without another word, I pushed through the front door and hurried up the stairs, my footsteps echoing off the walls of the narrow corridor. When I reached the room at the top of the stairs, I found Dixon standing by the bed, his figure cast in dim, grayish light. His face was uncharacteristically pale, his jaw set in a tight line as he adjusted a peculiar set of scientific apparatus on the table beside him.

"Dixon..." I started, but the sight of the room stole the words from me.

The stench struck me first—a harsh, acrid smell of ozone and singed metal, tinged with something foul, something rotten. It clung to the air, the metallic tang of burnt wiring mixing with the musty damp of old wood and sweat. The room itself was a scene of chaos and ruin.

The bed was unmade, its sheets rumpled and stained with something dark and sticky, a substance that had soaked into the fabric like ink spilled from a broken bottle. Cables snaked across the mattress, their rubber casings partially melted in places, the exposed copper filaments giving off a faint, eerie glow. An array of glass vacuum tubes, some intact, others shattered, were scattered across the floor, their broken edges glinting like teeth in the dim lamplight.

At the heart of it all sat a box-like contraption, humming faintly, its surface charred and warped as though exposed to intense heat. A row of delicate brass dials lined one side, their faces cracked, the needles frozen in unnatural positions. A series of levers jutted out, stiff and motionless, their polished surfaces dulled by a fine layer of soot. The device exhaled a low, rhythmic clicking, a mechanical death rattle that sent a shiver through me.

And then there was the coil.

A large copper coil, wound so tightly it seemed ready to snap, lay partially collapsed at the foot of the bed. It was still smoldering, a thin wisp of blue-white smoke curling from its center. The coil had fused at the core, a crystallised residue pooling at its base, the remnants of some unnatural reaction. My eyes followed the thick iron cables leading from it, which ended at a pair of restraints bolted to the bed frame.

Dixon looked up, his eyes meeting mine with an expression I couldn't read.

"It was getting weaker," he said, his voice strangely subdued. "It just... stopped functioning."

The detached tone in his voice disturbed me, and I took a step closer, glancing over the strange setup on the bed.

"What was it, Dixon?" I asked, though part of me dreaded the answer.

Dixon gestured vaguely at the bed, as though the remnants lying there required no further explanation. "I never managed to solve the problem of entropy within its core. The structure degraded too rapidly. But there's no need for sorrow, Paul," he added, his gaze hardening as if he were chastising me. "You don't cry over a machine, and you certainly don't give it a state funeral. You do eat meat, don't you?"

I stared at him, trying to process what he'd said. He spoke of the creature so clinically, as though it were nothing more than a broken clock. But the image of the stretcher, of the white-covered form being carried away, lingered in my mind.

Before I could respond, Dixon adjusted the brass dials on his apparatus with precise, deliberate movements—too deliberate. His fingers, usually so steady, hesitated for a fraction of a second over one of the switches, as though caught in some private thought before he corrected himself and continued. His jaw tensed, ever so slightly, and he exhaled through his nose, a controlled breath that didn't quite mask the way his hand clenched before retreating into his coat pocket. The movement was small, almost imperceptible, but it told me more than his words ever could. Beneath the sharp lines of his reasoning, something unsettled him—something he would never admit, perhaps even to himself.

"But Dixon... Was the machine sentient?" I started, my voice uncertain, wanting to argue, to somehow make him understand that there was something deeply troubling about the whole affair.

"White, you don't even know whether I am sentient or not. Even if I were, what if I felt your pain as pleasure and your pleasure as pain, saw your red as blue and your blue as red? Surely you don't cry over the enemies of the Empire—the Mahdists, the Burmese rebels..."

"You know full well that that machine was no enemy of the Empire."

"Granted. Neither was the unfortunate cow, whose steak you devoured for dinner yesterday evening—out of necessity, my friend, not out of malice."

"Was there really any necessity?"

Before I could find the words, Dixon's hand shot out, and I found two slips of paper pressed into my palm.

"Please, White. Let's change the subject. I'm well aware of the imperfections in my work. I need to take my mind off it. Here," he said briskly, "I've secured us tickets to a performance by someone called 'the Mechanist'. It's at the George Tavern. Starts in less than an hour."

I looked down at the tickets, feeling the sharp corners dig into my hand. "The Mechanist?"

"Yes," he replied, his tone already shifting back to his usual calm, brisk demeanour. "A magician, of sorts. Supposedly, he has machines of his own, devices that defy logic. Rumour has it he's an engineer as much as he is a showman. I thought it might be worth our time to see if he has any genuine skill or if he's merely another charlatan."

I wanted to press him further about the "failed experiment", to make him explain the strange scene I'd walked into. But there was a glint in Dixon's eye, a spark of curiosity that seemed to dispel the pallor of his face. I could tell he'd already compartmentalised the incident, filed it away as an unfortunate but necessary step in his pursuit of knowledge.

"Come on, Paul," he said, nodding toward the door. "We don't want to be late."

With a reluctant nod, I pocketed the tickets and followed him out. But as we descended the staircase, I couldn't shake the image of the black carriage, the two men, and the blanketed body. The echoes of Shaw's lecture, of determinism, of chaos, lingered in my mind.

And as we stepped into the fog-filled streets, I couldn't help but wonder if Dixon's curiosity might one day lead him—and me—into a darkness beyond anything we could comprehend. Perhaps the chain of events that will lead us to that darkness has been put in place already, much like Shaw's deterministic meteorological phenomena.

Chapter 3
The Mechanist

Dixon and I arrived at the George Tavern, the weathered sign hanging above the door swaying slightly in the night breeze.

Few public houses in London command such renown—or indeed, such infamy—as the George Tavern. Though the present structure dates to the 1820s, it retains the original brickwork of the old Halfway House, an establishment immortalised in the writings of Chaucer, Pepys, and Dickens. Situated along the well-trodden road to the London Docks, the inn once flourished due to its adjoining botanic garden, where exotic flora, imported from the farthest reaches of the Empire, were cultivated with great care.

Yet, perhaps the greatest marvel of all lies not in the histories recorded, nor in the gardens once tended, but in the view granted to those who venture to the attic of the George. There, high above the city's labyrinthine streets, the traveller may look out over green fields stretching to the river, where the masts of great ships rise like sentinels against the sky—silent witnesses to the ceaseless tide of London's fortune.

Tonight the air buzzed with an expectant energy, a kind of thrill that seemed to electrify the patrons streaming in and out. The George was already crowded, its dimly lit corners alive with the chatter of men and women who had come to see the mysterious Mechanist perform. As we pushed our way through, Dixon glanced around the pub with a look of quiet appraisal, his gaze sharp and discerning.

The performance was being held upstairs, where an improvised stage had been arranged. I followed Dixon up the narrow staircase, and as we entered the room, my eyes were immediately drawn to the figure of the Mechanist himself. He was a tall, statuesque man dressed in an Inverness cape, his face obscured by a Venetian mask that glinted under the gaslights. Beside him stood a young woman, his assistant, whose elegance was matched only by the air of mystery she exuded. Together, they looked like something out of a fevered dream—a vision both theatrical and unsettling.

Dixon nudged me, his gaze fixed on the mechanical equipment arrayed on the stage. Intricate gears and levers glinted in the light, and tubes ran from one apparatus to another, snaking across the stage in an arrangement that seemed too elaborate for a mere performance. Dixon's eyes narrowed as he studied the setup, his lips pressed into a thin line.

The Mechanist began his act with a dramatic flourish, extending a gloved hand to the audience. His voice was deep, commanding, with a slight foreign accent that only added to his mystique.

"I require a volunteer," he announced, sweeping his gaze over the audience. A few murmurs went through the crowd until a young woman near the front of the room rose, her cheeks flushed with excitement.

"Your name, my dear?" the Mechanist asked, his voice velvet-smooth.

"Mary," she replied, smiling nervously.

"And your age?"

"Twenty-one," she said, a touch of pride in her voice.

The Mechanist offered her a chair, gesturing for her to sit. She complied, her eyes bright with curiosity and a touch of apprehension. He spoke softly, his tone hypnotic.

"Close your eyes and raise your arms in front of you," he

instructed. "Imagine your left arm supporting a heavy pile of books, while light helium balloons are tied to your right."

Mary's arms began to move as if responding to invisible forces. Her left arm slowly sank, her right arm rose higher. The audience watched in rapt silence, their eyes wide with amazement.

"As your left arm touches your knee," the Mechanist continued in a low, calming tone, "you will enter a deep, restful sleep."

As if on cue, Mary's left arm lowered to her knee, and her head drooped, her body relaxing completely. The Mechanist wasted no time. He carefully affixed a strange apparatus to her head, a contraption resembling a helmet connected by wires to a cylindrical structure on stage.

I could not help but think of Franz Anton Mesmer as I watched the Mechanist weave his spectacle. Mesmer, the German physician turned mystic, had once captivated the courts of Europe with his peculiar theories of animal magnetism—a force, he claimed, that flowed through all living and inanimate matter alike. He insisted that ailments of the body and mind could be cured by manipulating this unseen energy, his hands guiding it like an orchestra conductor shaping invisible currents.

The idea, as preposterous as it now seems to modern science, held sway for decades. From the salons of Paris to the drawing rooms of Vienna, mesmerism found its adherents—those who swore by its power, those who sought in its hypnotic trances an answer to ailments no doctor could remedy. Even as the century progressed and scientific rigour dismantled his grand assertions, Mesmer's influence lingered. The Scottish surgeon James Braid, in the 1840s, would strip the practice of its mystical trappings and rechristen it as hypnotism, though the fascination with trance-like states remained much the same.

It is an amusing irony that Mesmer, this great mystifier of men, was himself a great patron of the arts. He counted Haydn and Mozart among his acquaintances, and it was said that he believed music to hold its own mesmeric qualities—a harmony of vibrations that could soothe the afflicted mind, much like his famed treatments.

Watching the Mechanist with his gloved hands, his voice measured and commanding, I could not help but feel that I was witnessing a descendant of Mesmer's peculiar craft. Was this not the same performance—the art of suggestion, the clever manipulation of expectation, the blurring of science and spectacle?

And yet, what happened next was so utterly unexpected and terrifying that all my thoughts of Mesmer's well-intentioned charlatanism vanished without a trace. The Mechanist was no Mesmer but something else entirely.

With a flourish, his assistant walked across the stage toward the table, her movements deliberate, almost reverent. She gripped the black cloth with gloved fingers, then, in a single motion, whisked it away. Beneath it sat a glass cylinder, tall and gleaming under the gaslights. And within the cylinder—suspended in a clear, viscous fluid—was a human head.

The sight struck me like a physical blow. My breath caught in my throat, and I felt my stomach lurch violently. The head's pale, waxen skin gleamed under the stage lights, too smooth, too perfect in its stillness. The lips hung slightly open, as though the severed mouth had been caught in the middle of some final, breathless word. The eyes—God, the eyes—were half-lidded, revealing dull, unseeing whites beneath sunken lids. They looked damp, swollen, as though the fluid had preserved them just enough to prevent them from shriveling into true death. The dark hair floated in the liquid, swaying ever so slightly, a grotesque mimicry of life.

A wave of cold nausea gripped me. I had seen death

before—the open caskets of the unfortunate, the pale faces of the drowned hauled from the Thames—but never like this. Never so intimate, never so perverse. It was as if the Mechanist had stolen this poor soul from the grave and forced it to endure one final, hideous performance.

The audience had fallen into a stunned silence, the murmurs of excitement evaporating in an instant. I heard a woman's sharp intake of breath somewhere behind me, followed by the dull thud of a fainting body hitting the floor. Gaslight flickered against the jar's smooth surface, sending refracted shadows dancing over the Mechanist's masked face. He stood beside the head, his posture poised, expectant, as if he were waiting—no, savouring—the audience's collective horror.

Dixon, beside me, remained motionless, his jaw set tight, his gaze locked onto the grisly display. A muscle twitched at his temple, the only sign of his own reaction. But I could feel it—the tension in the air between us, a shared revulsion, though Dixon's expression was more analytical than mine. He was studying it. Calculating.

The Mechanist let the moment stretch, his gloved fingers reaching out to adjust something on the cylinder. His assistant stood at his side, her face unreadable, her gaze lowered. Slowly, he turned a brass dial at the base of the glass jar.

A hiss.

Bubbles rose in the liquid, spiraling around the submerged head like tiny beads of quicksilver. Then, impossibly, the eyelids fluttered.

I stiffened, gripping the edge of my chair so hard my fingers ached. Surely, I had imagined it. Some trick of the light, some distortion from the fluid. But no—there it was again. A flicker. A movement.

The lips twitched, parting ever so slightly.

The Mechanist leaned forward, his masked face close to the glass. His voice was smooth, deliberate. But this time he was addressing his words not to Mary but to the severed head.

"Name?"

A silence. A breathless, unbearable moment of stillness.

Then, in a low, wet whisper, the severed head replied, its voice wet and rattling, like air forced through ruined lungs. The lips parted with a slow, unnatural hesitation, as if the tendons and muscles, long surrendered to death, were resisting some unseen force compelling them back to life. The jaw moved sluggishly, with a grotesque, mechanical stiffness, the skin at the corners of the mouth stretching taut before snapping back like aged parchment. Then came the voice—a low, rattling whisper, thick with something wet and glutinous, like air forced through waterlogged lungs. It did not sound like speech, not in any natural sense. It was distorted, hollow, as though emerging from deep within a cavern, yet unmistakably human. A shudder crawled up my spine, my breath catching in my throat. My rational mind screamed for an explanation—ventriloquism, some concealed mechanism—but deep in my gut, a colder, more primal fear took hold. This was wrong. Every instinct rebelled against what my senses were telling me. The dead did not speak. And yet, this one had.

"Mary."

A gasp rippled through the audience. My own breath caught in my throat. The head—the thing—had spoken in a woman's voice.

I turned sharply to Dixon, but he gave no indication of shock. If anything, he looked more interested now, his eyes narrowing in keen scrutiny. He murmured under his breath, just barely audible over the stunned hush of the room.

"Electricity... or resonance? No... no, that shouldn't be possible."

I could barely hear him. My thoughts were tumbling too fast, my body stiff with something between horror and cold, morbid fascination. I didn't want to watch. And yet I could not tear my gaze away.

The Mechanist continued, his voice calm, measured. "Age?"

"Twenty-one," the head rasped, the words emerging like a sigh of wind through a cracked door.

A shudder passed through me. That voice—somehow, it was not coming from the Mechanist, nor from any hidden accomplice. It came from the lips in the jar.

The glass seemed to darken, the formaldehyde taking on an almost sickly hue as the bubbles swirled. The assistant adjusted something on the side of the apparatus, her hands deft and precise, and the voice wavered, almost faltering.

"Where were you born?"

The head hesitated. Just for a fraction of a second.

Then, just as before, it answered.

"Bethnal Green."

The Mechanist's lips curled into a small smile. "Are you betrothed, Mary?"

"Yes," the head murmured, the answer leaving the audience in a stunned hush.

The Mechanist tilted his head, as if savoring the moment. "And the name of your fiancé?"

"Jonathan Wilkins," the head answered, the voice faint but unmistakable.

As the name left its lips, the assistant moved quickly, draping a cloth over the jar. The head was obscured once more, and with a snap of his fingers, the Mechanist seemed to rouse the young woman from her trance. Mary's eyes fluttered open, and she looked around, dazed, as if she had awoken from a dream.

The Mechanist turned to her. "Tell us, Mary, where were you born?"

Mary blinked, seemingly confused by the question, but after a pause, she reiterated the information that the audience had already learned from the severed head.

"And," he said with a slight smile, "are you due to marry Jonathan Wilkins?"

At this, Mary's cheeks flushed a brilliant red. She gasped, covering her mouth with her hand before bolting from her chair and rushing toward the door, vanishing into the crowd with a murmur of hushed voices trailing after her.

The applause was thunderous, the audience caught in a frenzy of awe and disbelief. The Mechanist held up his hand, and just as he did, a dark shape flitted past the window. Another followed, then another. Bats—dozens of them—flew into the room, their wings beating wildly as they circled above the audience. The room erupted into screams, people ducking and covering their heads as the bats swooped down. Women shrieked, men cursed, and the Mechanist, with a calm and almost sinister smile, pulled a lever on his equipment. As if obeying his command, the bats surged toward the window and disappeared into the night.

Once the room had settled, he gestured to his assistant to select another volunteer. The assistant's gaze swept the crowd before settling on me. She approached, her expression inscrutable as she reached out, placing a hand on my cheek. Then, before I could react, she plucked a few strands of hair from my head, holding them delicately between her fingers as she brought them to the Mechanist.

The Mechanist, with a flourish, struck a match and held one of the hairs to the flame. I felt a strange heat at the crown of my head, and before I could comprehend what was happening, a fierce pain shot through my scalp.

My hand flew to my head as I realised—my hair was on fire.

Dixon reacted instantly, throwing his jacket over my head and smothering the flames. The sudden sensation left me reeling, my heart pounding as I yanked the jacket away, glancing up just in time to see the Mechanist and his assistant slip behind the curtain.

The lights dimmed, and when the curtain rose again, the stage was empty.

The crowd erupted once more, the room filled with excited chatter, and Dixon took my arm, guiding me toward the exit. As we descended the stairs and stepped back into the cool night air, I felt the pulse of the crowd's energy lingering around us, their applause echoing in my ears.

I saw Dixon's face above me, clinically studying the painful burn on my scalp. "*Panem et circenses*," he sighed at last. That didn't help.

"You will be alright." That was slightly more encouraging.

"What just happened?" I asked, glancing back at Dixon, who seemed remarkably unfazed.

"It appears," he replied, his tone thoughtful, "that we have a rather unusual case on our hands. This Mechanist... there's something disturbingly authentic about his performance. Not merely theatrics. Something more."

Dixon helped me to my feet. We stood in silence, each lost in thought, the strange spectacle replaying in my mind. The talking head, the bats, the burning hair—it was all too bizarre, too surreal. But beneath the thrill of it, a dark suspicion lingered, a question that gnawed at me with every step we took away from the George Tavern.

Just what was the Mechanist trying to accomplish—and what secrets lay behind that mask?

Chapter 4
A Lead

Dixon's eyes had taken on that keen, determined glint I knew too well, and without so much as a pause after the performance, he signaled for me to follow him. We made our way through the dispersing crowd, weaving around clusters of patrons still abuzz with excitement, their conversations filled with snippets of disbelief and admiration for the Mechanist's strange feats. Dixon ignored them all, his gaze fixed on the small doorway leading to the back of the George Tavern.

"Dixon, what exactly are you doing?" I asked, half-knowing the answer already but reluctant to believe he was about to pursue this obsession further.

"Making a small inquiry," he replied with an air of determination. "I intend to learn more about this Mechanist and, ideally, how he achieves such 'miracles'."

We reached a side door marked "Private", and Dixon, without hesitation, knocked firmly. A moment later, it opened, revealing a wiry, gray-haired man who looked us up and down with a mixture of curiosity and suspicion. I recognised him as the tavern's manager, the man who had been orchestrating the flow of patrons and overseeing the evening's events.

"Can I help you?" he asked in a guarded tone.

"Yes, I certainly hope so," Dixon said smoothly, slipping into a calm and measured voice that he often used when negotiating with more difficult parties. "My name is Professor

Reginald Dixon, and I am something of an admirer of your performer, the Mechanist. His work fascinates me. Might I trouble you for his contact information? I would like to extend him an invitation to a gathering of like-minded intellectuals and artists."

The manager's eyes narrowed, and he crossed his arms, leaning back slightly as though to place some physical distance between us. He looked Dixon up and down with a shrewd gaze, clearly weighing his options. A faint, knowing smile curled at the corners of his mouth.

"Admire him, do you?" he said, his tone edged with skepticism. "And where exactly might you be an 'admirer' from, Professor Dixon? Are you, perhaps, in the business yourself?"

Dixon's expression didn't waver, but I could sense his irritation. "I am not in any form of public entertainment, if that's what you're suggesting. My interest is purely academic."

"Purely academic, is it?" The manager gave a small, derisive chuckle. "Forgive me, Professor, but I hear that line often enough from other 'admirers' looking to book acts of their own. The Mechanist's business here is his own, and it stays that way."

"Perhaps I haven't made myself clear," Dixon said, his voice hardening slightly. "This is not about bookings or performances. I am genuinely interested in the Mechanist's methods. I can assure you, my intentions are entirely professional."

But the manager remained unmoved, his suspicion deepening with each word Dixon spoke. He shifted his weight, tilting his head and giving Dixon a closer, more piercing look.

"With all due respect, Professor," he said finally, "I don't know you from Adam, and I have a duty to keep the Mechanist's affairs private. He works alone, no apprentices, no assistants—not outside the ones you see on stage, that is. We get plenty of inquiries from men who say they're admirers, but they all want the same thing—his secrets. And the Mechanist...

well, he's not the type to take kindly to those prying into his work."

Dixon's face remained composed, but I could sense a thin thread of frustration behind his eyes. He adjusted his stance, clearing his throat with an air of composure that masked his rising irritation.

"I understand your loyalty to your performer," Dixon said, his tone carefully controlled. "But rest assured, I am no rival impresario. My only interest in the Mechanist's work lies in understanding his... unconventional methods. He possesses a remarkable talent that would be of great interest to my research."

But the manager remained steadfast, his expression unyielding. "Perhaps that's true, Professor. But I have no interest in getting into whatever research you're doing. Now, if there's nothing else, I have business to attend to."

He stepped back, his hand moving toward the door to shut it.

Dixon hesitated, clearly debating whether to push further, but something in the manager's stare warned him against it. With a curt nod, Dixon took a step back, and I followed as he led us out of the dim corridor.

Once outside in the open air, Dixon's expression betrayed a flicker of irritation that he quickly masked.

"He's not what he seems, this Mechanist," Dixon muttered under his breath, his eyes narrowed with a gleam of suspicion. "There is more to his performance than mere spectacle."

"Clearly," I replied, still shaken by what we'd witnessed. "But perhaps there's a reason he guards his methods so closely. What would you do if you had access to his work?"

Dixon didn't respond, his gaze fixed somewhere in the distance. I could see the wheels turning in his mind, his curiosity now piqued to a degree that worried me. For Dixon, this was no longer just a performance to marvel at. It was a puzzle—

one he was determined to solve.

Dixon and I barely made it through the front door of the George Tavern before he signaled for me to follow him back upstairs. His movements were sharp, urgent, as if he'd uncovered something that simply couldn't wait.

When we reached the upper floor again, we were met with an unusual sight. Two stocky Italian porters—identical twins by the look of them—were packing the Mechanist's equipment with remarkable precision. They worked in perfect synchrony, moving like reflections of one another as they dismantled the apparatus that had so captivated the audience only minutes before.

Dixon approached them without hesitation. "Pardon me," he said, his voice smooth yet edged with authority, "where are you taking this equipment?"

The twins paused, exchanged a glance, and then went right back to their task, ignoring him entirely. Dixon's eyes narrowed, and he reached into his pocket, pulling out what appeared to be a banknote, holding it out casually but conspicuously.

The sight of money didn't have the effect Dixon had intended. One of the twins glanced down at it, then muttered something in Italian to his brother. Before I could decipher their response, the twin called out, "Antonio!"

A third man appeared from the staircase—a figure who looked exactly like the other two. Triplets.

Antonio strode over, and the other two fell back, watching him with deference. He was clearly the leader, and he regarded us with a cool, assessing gaze, folding his arms over his chest.

"What is it you want?" Antonio asked, his English laced with a heavy accent.

Dixon didn't miss a beat. "We're admirers of the Mechanist's work. I merely wished to speak to him—offer a compliment or two, perhaps ask a question."

Antonio's eyes narrowed. "The Mechanist doesn't care for admirers who pry," he said flatly. "And we've been told to keep his work secure. No one interferes with his equipment." He looked pointedly at the banknote Dixon was still holding. "You can keep your money."

Before Dixon or I could respond, the triplets moved in unison. They seized us, their grips like iron, and marched us down the hallway. Within seconds, we were unceremoniously shoved into the pub manager's office, the heavy door slamming shut behind us. The pub manager stood in the room, hands on his hips, a faint sneer on his lips.

"Ah, Professor Dixon and his... assistant," the manager said, a dangerous gleam in his eyes. "Seems you're both more curious than is good for you."

Dixon's expression remained steely. "Curiosity is the heart of all progress," he replied, unfazed. "Surely a man of your station could understand that."

"Progress?" The manager chuckled, but there was no humor in it. "The only progress you'll be making is out of this pub, and maybe with a few broken bones if I get my way."

With that, he reached for the door, glancing back at us with a look that made my stomach churn. "Stay here," he said. "I'll be right back with a bit of help."

The door slammed shut, and I heard the click of the lock. I looked at Dixon, my mind racing with panic. "What now?" I whispered, trying to keep my voice steady.

Dixon surveyed the room quickly, his eyes sharp and calculating. He walked to the window, lifting the latch and peering down. "We'll have to improvise," he said, motioning for me to join him. "Come on, Paul. Unless you prefer to await whatever 'help' our friend intends to bring."

I needed no further urging. We managed to slip out through the narrow window and onto the roof, Dixon leading the way as we scrambled over to a nearby chimney. As I held my breath, he edged down the brickwork, signaling for me to follow. With one last glance toward the office door, I dropped down beside him, moving as quietly as I could.

But as we reached the street, I saw them. The pub manager, the triplets, and a handful of burly men were already moving toward us, their footsteps heavy and deliberate. I felt my heart hammering in my chest as Dixon grabbed my arm, pulling me into a sprint.

We tore down the fog-drenched streets of Stepney, the sounds of our pursuers' shouts echoing through the night. The narrow alleys and twisting lanes closed in around us, dark shadows stretching like clawed fingers in the gaslight. I tried to keep up with Dixon, my breathing ragged, while his pace never faltered, his movements fluid and assured.

Finally, we ducked into a narrow alleyway, pressing ourselves against the wall as we listened to the footsteps passing close by. I glanced over at Dixon, surprised to see him so composed, even here in the depths of Stepney.

"You know your way around here," I whispered, astonished.

Dixon offered a slight smile, though his eyes remained fixed on the street. "You pick up a few tricks along the way," he replied simply.

The footsteps faded, and I let out a sigh of relief, but my mind was still racing, replaying the night's events. "So, that's it then?" I said bitterly. "We're left with nothing but questions. We'll never find out who this Mechanist is or what he's up to."

Dixon's smile widened a fraction, and he reached into his coat pocket, producing a slip of paper. "Never say never, Paul."

He held up the paper, and I could just make out the words in the dim light: it was an invoice, printed neatly with the address of the George Tavern, and above it, "Pinoli's Restaurant, Little Italy, Soho."

"You stole this?" I asked, astonished.

Dixon tucked the invoice back into his pocket, his expression unreadable. “I’ve borrowed it for the purposes of our investigation. I thought it might come in handy. Looks like the Mechanist has left us a trail after all.”

For a moment, I was speechless. Dixon had anticipated this, perhaps even planned for it, his mind working several steps ahead as always. I couldn’t help but feel a thrill of excitement—mixed with a fair dose of trepidation—as I realised we weren’t finished with the Mechanist just yet.

Chapter 5
The Dark Flat

Soho had long since secured its reputation as one of London's principal centres of entertainment. There had long been a tradition of public amusement in these streets, stretching back to the 1690s, when dancing schools first appeared on Frith Street.

Pinoli's Restaurant was every bit as charming as it looked from the outside. The warm, inviting aroma of garlic and herbs filled the air, masking the undercurrent of mystery that had brought us here. Dixon and I were led to a small table near the back, where Pinoli himself—a round, amiable man with slicked-back hair—greeted us with a knowing smile. When Dixon tried to inquire about the Mechanist, Pinoli merely chuckled and insisted that we dine before he would say anything more.

Reluctantly, Dixon agreed. We ate in tense silence, though the food was excellent—plates of rich pasta, tender meats, and roasted vegetables, all prepared with exquisite detail. Finally, as we finished, Pinoli returned to the table, an expectant look in his eyes.

"Tell me, gentlemen, how was your meal?" he asked, almost too politely.

Dixon took the opportunity to lean forward, his tone deceptively casual. "We've heard of a certain gentleman staying here, known in certain circles as the Mechanist. An entertainer, a gentleman of magical inclination."

Pinoli's smile widened, though his eyes held a glint of something darker. "Ah, yes. Signor Bartolomeo Bertini," he said. "A gentleman from Italy, skilled in the art of magic. He has indeed taken a flat upstairs."

With our suspicions confirmed, Dixon thanked Pinoli, and we rose from the table. We followed a narrow, creaking staircase at the back of the restaurant, the air growing colder with each step. A damp chill lingered here, as if the warmth of the kitchen never quite reached the upper floors. The walls were tight, pressing in on either side, and the stairwell seemed impossibly narrow.

I ran my hand along the railing, my fingers brushing against something slick—perhaps a varnish, or something else I dared not consider. A whisper of unease prickled at my skin. "This stairwell is impossibly narrow. How could the Mechanist have transported his equipment up here?" I whispered to Dixon.

Dixon, ever determined, only nodded, dismissing my concerns.

At last, we reached the top landing. A single door stood ahead of us, its frame warped, as though the wood had expanded and shrunk with time, absorbing the moisture of years. The brass handle was dull, untouched by polish or care. A faint, rancid scent seeped through the cracks.

Dixon hesitated only briefly before pressing the door open.

The smell hit us first.

A thick, metallic stench, cloying and wrong—like rust and old meat left too long in stagnant water. My stomach twisted as the acrid scent filled my nostrils, and I fought the urge to gag.

Dixon struck a match, and in the weak, flickering glow, the horror revealed itself.

In the center of the room lay a body, sprawled on its back. Headless.

The corpse was clad in a fine Italian suit, monogrammed with the initials BB embroidered onto the breast pocket in gold thread. Bartolomeo Bertini. The Mechanist. Or at least, what remained of him.

My throat tightened. The body was oddly pristine, no signs of violence beyond the grotesque absence of its head. The skin was pallid, waxen, drained entirely of blood. There was no splatter, no mess—only the eerie stillness of a thing long dead. It was unnatural, too clean, as if it had been preserved.

Dixon knelt beside the corpse, peering closely in the dim light. His brow furrowed. "No blood," he murmured. "The body is dry. This wasn't done recently." He reached out, hesitated, then touched the stiff fabric of the suit. "Rigor has passed. Days, perhaps, yet..." His voice trailed off.

I swallowed hard. The air was thick with silence, an oppressive quiet that pressed against my ears. My pulse thundered beneath my skin.

And then—

Footsteps.

Slow. Deliberate.

Ascending the staircase.

My body was locked in place. A cold dread settled in my gut.

Dixon's match flickered, the light dancing wildly against the walls. Without a word, he pinched it out, plunging us into darkness.

The footsteps stopped just outside the door.

A long, breathless pause.

Then, a voice—low, mocking, impossibly near.

"Did you think you could simply walk away?"

The words slithered through the air like smoke, curling into my ears, sinking into my bones.

I felt Dixon tense beside me. I barely dared to breathe.

Chapter 6
Prisoners

Newgate Prison, situated at the corner of Newgate Street and Old Bailey, stands at the very heart of London's history, its grim walls bearing witness to the city's most infamous criminals, its most desperate wretches, and its most wretched failures of justice.

Dixon and I were escorted to a waiting carriage, flanked by constables on either side. The journey was short and silent, the cobblestones jarring beneath us, each turn taking us deeper into London's heart.

I felt as though I were being swallowed whole by the city itself. The buildings loomed taller, the streets darker, the air thick with the stench of the Thames, coal smoke, and something fouler—something unmistakably human.

Dixon maintained his composure, but I felt my heart sink.

When we stopped, I saw the imposing façade of the prison rising before us, its dark, looming stone walls seeming to swallow the light.

Inside, we were separated immediately.

I was led down a narrow hallway, the sounds of chains and murmured voices echoing off the cold stone. A constable opened a door to a small room and gestured for me to enter.

The room into which I was thrown was narrow and rank with mildew. The door clanged shut behind me with a finality that turned my stomach.

I sat alone, my mind racing, until an inspector entered.

The inspector was a gaunt man with steel-gray whiskers and eyes like chips of flint. He settled himself across from me at a scarred wooden table, producing a leather-bound notebook and a steel-nibbed pen with methodical precision.

"State your name for the record," he commanded, his voice carrying the clipped authority of one accustomed to obedience.

"Paul White, sir. Student at the Royal College of Science."

"And your association with Reginald Dixon?"

"He is my mentor, sir. I assist with his research and attend his lectures."

The inspector's pen scratched across the paper. "You were discovered in the company of the said Dixon at premises above Pinoli's Restaurant, in the presence of a decapitated corpse. Explain yourself."

I straightened in my chair, trying to project calm I did not feel. "We had tracked the performer known as the Mechanist to those lodgings, sir. We were investigating his activities when we discovered the body."

"Investigating." The word dripped with skepticism. "On whose authority?"

"Our own, sir. Academic authority, that is. Professor Dixon suspected the Mechanist of employing dangerous scientific methods in his performances."

The inspector leaned forward, his gaze boring into mine. "So you admit to unlawful entry?"

"The door was unlocked, sir. We entered to—"

"To what? Plant evidence? Remove it?"

My throat constricted. "Certainly not, sir. We were as shocked as anyone to find—"

"Did you know the victim?"

"We did not, sir. We had no involvement in that man's death."

"Yet you admit to being present when the body was

discovered. You admit to unlawful entry. You admit to a close association with the accused." The inspector's pen hovered over his notebook like a weapon. "What did Dixon instruct you to do with the evidence?"

"Nothing, sir. He gave me no such instructions."

"Come now, Mr. White. A young man of your station does not simply stumble upon dismembered corpses. What was Dixon's true purpose in that flat?"

The walls seemed to press closer. My hands had begun to tremble, and I clasped them tightly in my lap. "I have told you the truth, sir."

"The truth?" The inspector's laugh was cold. "The truth is that you and Dixon broke into those premises with criminal intent. The truth is that Dixon has a reputation for unsavory associations and questionable experiments."

"That is not–"

"The truth is that an innocent man lies dead, and you protect his killer!"

The accusation struck me like a physical blow. "Professor Dixon is not a killer!"

"Then explain the evidence!" The inspector's voice rose to a roar that echoed off the stone walls.

My composure cracked like ice in spring. "I don't know! I cannot explain it, but I know Dixon had nothing to do with it!"

"You're lying to protect him. What hold does he have over you? What has he promised you?"

"Nothing! He has been nothing but honourable–"

"Honourable men do not consort with criminals and charlatans!"

"He was investigating–"

"He was plotting! And you, Mr. White, are either his accomplice or his fool!"

Tears of frustration burned my eyes. "I will not betray an

innocent man, no matter what you accuse me of."

The inspector sat back, studying me with cold calculation. "Your loyalty is touching, if misplaced. But mark me well, young man—your Professor Dixon will hang for this crime, and your silence will not save him. And you... you are also on your way to the gallows, a precarious path. Do you think your master will protect you the way you are protecting him? You are deluding yourself. Something to ponder, Mr. White."

I met his gaze as steadily as I could manage. "Then so be it, sir. I have nothing more to say."

The inspector closed his notebook with a sharp snap. "We shall see about that."

Once they finished with me, I was led out and saw Dixon, who looked equally drained but composed. The officers moved us through a labyrinthine series of corridors until we arrived at the main holding area of Newgate Prison.

The prison was a sprawling fortress of grim corridors and damp cells, filled with the stench of despair. Iron bars lined each cell, casting shadows that seemed to stretch and distort in the dim light. The walls were cold and damp, the air thick with the oppressive scent of rot and neglect.

We were led to separate cells. Mine was a narrow, claustrophobic space with barely enough room to move. The walls were scratched and chipped, each mark a testament to the prisoners who had languished here before me. I gripped the iron bars, my hands trembling as I looked down the hallway, straining to catch a glimpse of Dixon.

The cell door clanged shut behind me, and I was left alone in the dimness, the flickering gaslight barely illuminating the small space. The sound of distant footsteps echoed through the halls, mingling with the soft moans and mutters of other prisoners. Fear gnawed at me, the reality of our situation settling over me like a weight.

The hours—or was it days?—that followed were a slow,

creeping nightmare. The cold gnawed at my bones, the iron bars cut into my palms as I gripped them, desperate for some connection to the outside world. Shadows stretched long and jagged from the torchlight flickering in the corridor, the distorted figures of gaolers moving like wraiths. The sounds of Newgate became an oppressive symphony: the scratching of vermin in the straw, the rattle of chains, the murmurs of madmen speaking to ghosts.

I had known fear before, but this—this was something else. This was isolation in its truest, cruelest form. The weight of history pressed down upon me. How many men had sat in this very cell, waiting for justice that would never come? How many had stared at these same walls in the final hours before their execution, their names soon to be forgotten, lost in the damp stone and the rot?

And who, in this vast and indifferent city, would care enough to help me?

Where were the hallowed halls of the Royal College of Science? Where was the terrifying but almost cozily familiar world of the Docklands? My scientific career was at its inception, but now I'd gone and thrown it all away.

Why did I follow this strange man into the worst imaginable trap?

The gaslight flickered, then disappeared altogether. The darkness of my cell was most profound, a void so complete that I fancy it might swallow a man's very soul. In my desperation, I had taken to exploring the confines of my prison with naught but my trembling fingers. The stone was cold and damp beneath my touch, worn smooth by the passage of countless wretched souls before me.

It was during such an exploration that my fingertips discovered what appeared to be etchings upon the wall. Slowly, with mounting curiosity, I traced each character, each word, discerning through touch what my eyes could not perceive in this perpetual night.

A verse! Some poor wretch, perhaps occupying this very cell before my arrival, had carved his mournful poetry into the unyielding stone:

The hangman's noose,
The hangman's grin,
It's never loose,
It's always win,
If I could trim
The hangman's noose
It would be prim
And proper,
But reaper's grim,
As is his kin,
His evil twin,
The roper.

I withdrew my hand as though the wall had suddenly grown hot. A chill coursed through my frame, for in these crude lines I glimpsed the terror that had consumed my predecessor. How he must have sat, just as I do now, contemplating the hemp that would soon encircle his throat! What manner of courage—or perhaps madness—drove him to immortalise his dread in verse?

The thought of this unknown man, whose fingers once pressed against the same stone that now contained me, whose breath once filled this selfsame air, whose fate might soon be mine own... It overwhelmed my faculties. Was he innocent, as I professed to be? Did he, too, protest the injustice of his circumstance to unhearing ears? Did he weep, as I had wept, or did he meet his end with the stoic resignation that these verses suggest?

I traced the words once more, this nameless poet becoming

more real to me than the world beyond these walls. In his crude rhyme, I found a strange companionship amidst this solitude. We were brothers now, he and I, joined by stone and suffering, by the shadow of the gallows that loomed over us both.

Nothing now remained but the stench, the cold stone, the muffled moans of the other prisoners and the looming prospect of the undeserved gallows.

Each second filled with an unrelenting sense of dread. Every sound, every whisper seemed like it could be the beginning of something terrible. I knew Dixon was close, yet he felt worlds away, lost somewhere within the same dark labyrinth.

And who else did I have in this accursed city? Who would put in a word for me? Who would hold my hand?

My thoughts wandered to Alice, the barmaid whose acquaintance I had made some months previous. But I banished them, as it was almost sacrilege to think of her in this accursed abyss. But her face came back to me, and then there were images, fragments of my life in my native Bath. Then, eventually those fragments gave way to muffled shrieks and moans and the sound of water dripping on cold stone.

Was I asleep?

Just as the first rays of dawn pierced through the barred window, there was a sudden commotion. Footsteps approached, louder and more purposeful. My cell door swung open, and I blinked in the sudden flood of light.

Sir Edward Bradford himself entered, flanked by two officers. The Sir Edward Bradford. Commissioner of Police. His imposing figure cast a long shadow across the cell as he regarded me with a calm but penetrating gaze. Behind him, Dixon appeared, freed from his cell and standing beside the Commissioner.

Bradford inclined his head slightly, his voice a mix

of formality and something almost resembling respect. "Mr. White, Professor Dixon—I offer my apologies for this misunderstanding."

He gestured to the officers, who moved to escort us out. "Consider this a warning, gentlemen. Whatever game you're playing, tread carefully. Some mysteries were never meant to be solved. Professor Dixon, thank you for your services to the police."

With that, Bradford stepped back with quiet grace, allowing us to pass.

The door opened, and we stumbled forward, out of that wretched cell. As we left the confines of Newgate Prison and emerged into the pale morning light, Bradford's words echoed in my mind, casting a dark shadow over our next steps. Dixon and I exchanged a glance.

And for the first time since leaving Newgate, I breathed.

Chapter 7
Saeed's Visit

I hadn't slept a wink since that dreadful night, the events at Newgate replaying in my mind like a feverish vision. Bradford's cryptic warning, the headless body, the Mechanist's chilling performance—all of it churned together in my thoughts, leaving me both exhausted and restless.

I entered the living room to find Dixon seated at the table by the window, accompanied by Saeed, another of our fraternal order, the Brothers of Koach. They were engaged in a most methodical examination of yellowed newspapers from Dixon's considerable archive, their fingers carefully turning the delicate pages as though handling sacred texts.

"Paul," Dixon acknowledged my presence without raising his eyes from the newsprint. "We have made a discovery of some consequence."

I approached their table, observing the scattered papers bearing announcements of various entertainments and diversions.

"Behold," said Dixon, indicating with his forefinger a particular advertisement, "announcements of Bartolomeo Bertini's magical exhibitions from recent years. Several make mention of an apprentice by the name of Dominico."

Saeed, a man of Iraqi extraction whose intellect was matched only by his devotion to our cause, looked up at me with fevered eyes. "Dixon has formed a theory of considerable merit."

"Indeed," Dixon continued, stroking his whiskers thoughtfully. "I conjecture that this Dominico may very well be our Mechanist—the same villain who has dispatched his master, Bartolomeo Bertini, to his eternal reward."

Saeed's brow furrowed beneath his tarboosh. "What manner of motivation might drive such a man to such heinous acts?"

Dixon leaned back in his chair, his expression one of scholarly contemplation. "The Mechanist possesses extraordinary aptitude in matters scientific. And as is invariably the case, the primary impetus behind any scientist's endeavours is power." His lips curled into a sardonic smile. "It is hardly coincidental, gentlemen, that we ourselves are denominated the Brethren of Koach."

"But we employ our knowledge for benevolent purposes, not for wicked designs," Saeed protested with some agitation, his dark eyes flashing.

The conversation took an abrupt turn as Saeed's countenance fell. "I must report a domestic calamity of my own. My feline companion has vanished without trace."

At this juncture, I, who had been perusing the morning papers whilst their discourse continued, was struck by a most peculiar article.

"By heavens, gentlemen," I exclaimed, smoothing the newspaper upon the table. "You must attend to this extraordinary account. There has been a veritable stampede of cats in Stepney Green."

Their attention captured, I proceeded to read aloud the particulars of this bizarre occurrence.

"On the very night of the Mechanist's performance at the George Tavern, domestic felines were observed departing their residences in an inexplicable fashion. They joined in great numbers with other cats, forming a most unnatural procession moving en masse toward the river."

Dixon's eyes narrowed behind his spectacles. "And what became of these creatures?"

"Most extraordinary of all," I continued, "they attempted, quite against their nature, to traverse the Thames. The account describes scores of the poor creatures plunging into the murky waters, as though compelled by some invisible force."

Saeed's complexion paled visibly. "Then my Archimedes may have succumbed to this same mysterious influence."

As Saeed re-examined the article concerning the feline aberration, his attention was suddenly diverted to an adjacent column. His finger traced the lines of text with increasing urgency.

"Gentlemen, observe this," he exclaimed, his voice hushed yet intense. "General Alfred von Waldersee, who but a year past was relieved of his appointment, has been sighted in London."

I leaned forward to better view the article. "It states his visit was intended to be conducted in secrecy, yet several witnesses report having observed the General at The George Tavern on the very evening of the Mechanist's performance."

"A most curious coincidence," murmured Dixon, adjusting his spectacles.

"The German militarist is certainly no friend to the British Empire," I remarked, unable to conceal the suspicion in my tone. "One wonders what business brings such a man to our shores in so clandestine a fashion."

Dixon's fingers formed a steeple beneath his chin. "Indeed, most peculiar. A discharged German General, a mysterious mechanist, and a stampede of cats—all converging at a single location on a single evening." He paused, his expression grave. "Gentlemen, would it not be prudent to convene an emergency assembly of the Brethren of Koach?"

Saeed shifted uncomfortably in his chair. "Such a gathering would present considerable difficulties at present. The

Worshipful Master is abroad, and with the summer season upon us, many of our brethren have retired to their country estates." He adjusted his tarboosh with a practiced hand. "Though I have taken the liberty of informing him of our discoveries by telegram. Naturally, using the usual cipher."

Dixon nodded, acknowledging the wisdom in Saeed's words. His attention returned to the scattered newspapers, methodically examining each in turn. Suddenly, he drew a sharp breath.

"By all that is sacred," he exclaimed, thrusting a fresh newspaper toward us. "Observe this announcement."

I leaned forward to read the printed notice: "The Mechanist, Master of Scientific Wonders, shall present a Single Exhibition of Unprecedented Marvels at Alexandra Palace."

"The very edifice that rose from the ashes of the great fire," I murmured, recalling the palace's recent reconstruction following its destruction some years prior.

As I continued reading, another detail caught my attention. "It further states that Swami Saraswati himself shall bless the performance in the name of harmony and love."

Saeed's eyebrows rose markedly. "The Swami? His reputation precedes him. He has garnered quite a following among London's aristocratic circles, particularly amongst the ladies."

"Indeed," I remarked. "Lady Harrington-Smythe has transformed her conservatory into an Eastern temple for his private teachings, and the Duchess of Pemberton is said to have cancelled three separate engagements to attend his discourses on spiritual enlightenment."

Dixon gave a dismissive snort. "Another charlatan preying upon the credulity of bored society women. Though I confess the association with our Mechanist is most intriguing."

"What manner of harmony and love," Saeed pondered, "could possibly be embodied in the Mechanist's exhibitions? His performances have thus far culminated in rather disturbing spectacles."

Dixon's expression darkened. "I harbour considerable skepticism regarding the Mechanist's commitment to such lofty ideals, particularly in light of the gruesome nature of his demonstrations. The resurrection of Bertini's severed head at the George Tavern can scarcely be considered an act of benevolence."

"You and I must attend this performance," Dixon declared, his tone brooking no argument.

"Surely you cannot be serious," Saeed protested, his complexion ashen. "To place yourselves in such proximity to the Mechanist invites unnecessary peril. The villain and his confederates will undoubtedly recognise your persons."

A thin smile played across Dixon's lips. "My dear Saeed, there are aspects of my former profession with which you remain unacquainted. I was, in my younger days, considered something of a master in the art of disguise." He rose from his chair with newfound energy. "A skill which shall prove most serviceable on this particular occasion."

I exchanged glances with Saeed, who appeared far from convinced. For my part, I confess a curious mixture of trepidation and anticipation coursed through my veins at the prospect of confronting this mysterious Mechanist on his own ground.

A heavy silence descended upon the room as we contemplated the dark implications of these discoveries, the late morning sun casting long shadows across Dixon's collection of arcane knowledge.

Chapter 8
The Disguise

"You must understand, Paul, that the true art of disguise lies not merely in the alteration of one's garments, but in the fundamental transformation of one's entire aspect."

Dixon spoke with the authority of a master instructing his apprentice as he laid out an array of curious implements upon his mahogany dressing table. Our forthcoming expedition to Alexandra Palace had prompted him to reveal this particular talent from his mysterious past, a skill I confess I had not previously known him to possess.

"Pray observe," he continued, taking a small jar of what appeared to be theatrical greasepaint. "The human countenance possesses certain immutable features which the trained eye instinctively recognises. The distance between the eyes, for instance, and the prominence of the cheekbones."

With practiced fingers, he demonstrated upon his own visage. "One begins by establishing a foundation. Note how I apply this substance not merely as a covering, but as a means of reshaping the very architecture of my face."

I watched, fascinated, as Dixon's aristocratic features seemed to soften and blur beneath his ministrations. He worked methodically, explaining each step with scientific precision.

"The application of shadow creates the illusion of recession," he explained, darkening the area beneath his cheekbones.

"While highlighting produces the opposite effect. The human eye is readily deceived by such contrasts."

From a small leather case, he produced several curious implements: pieces of gutta-percha designed to alter the shape of the nose and cheeks, adhesive spirit gum, crepe hair, and spectacles of various designs.

"Now, you shall attempt the same," he directed, gesturing toward the chair before the looking glass.

Under his meticulous tutelage, I found myself being transformed. The sensation of the cold greasepaint upon my skin was most disagreeable, yet I submitted to Dixon's exacting instructions.

"No, no," he chided, correcting my clumsy efforts. "Apply it thus, with a stippling motion. You must build the illusion gradually."

For nearly an hour, we proceeded in this manner, Dixon demonstrating each technique before I attempted to replicate it. He showed me how false wrinkles could be created with judicious lines of burnt cork, how the apparent shape of one's eyes might be altered through the strategic application of shadow, and how dental appliances could transform the very shape of one's jaw.

"Now for the final elements of our disguises," Dixon announced, crossing to a large wardrobe from which he extracted two garments carefully wrapped in brown paper.

"Good heavens, Dixon," I exclaimed upon seeing the contents. "Surely you cannot be serious."

"I assure you, I am entirely in earnest," he replied, his expression betraying mild amusement at my discomfiture. "The most effective disguise is often that which places one in a social position rendering one effectively invisible to the casual observer."

The first bundle contained the complete ensemble of an elderly woman of modest means: a dark bombazine dress of outdated fashion, a shawl of faded tartan, gray cotton gloves darned at the fingers, and a bonnet adorned with artificial violets that had clearly seen better days.

"This shall be my attire," Dixon announced matter-of-factly. "The aged female relative is a figure who attracts little notice or suspicion, particularly when accompanied by a dutiful young relation."

From the second package emerged the unmistakable uniform of a public school boy: gray flannel trousers, a navy blazer bearing an embroidered crest, a cap of matching fabric, and a white collar of uncomfortable rigidity.

"And this, my dear Paul, shall be your disguise."

I regarded the garments with undisguised horror. "Dixon, I am twenty years of age. No one shall believe me a schoolboy."

"On the contrary," he replied with infuriating confidence. "With your slender build and the appropriate cosmetic adjustments, you shall present a most convincing portrait of a youth of sixteen or seventeen years. The casual observer sees what he expects to see, and nothing more."

What followed was a transformation so complete as to be scarcely credible. Dixon, that imposing figure of masculine intellect, disappeared entirely beneath the guise of a mild, elderly widow. His posture altered, his shoulders rounded, his hands acquired a slight tremor, and his voice emerged as a quavering treble when he spoke.

"Now, young Thomas," he addressed me in this unsettling falsetto, "do be a good lad and assist your grandmother with her shawl."

My own metamorphosis, while less dramatic, was no less thorough. The school uniform, which Dixon had obtained from some unspecified source, fitted with suspicious precision. My face, scrubbed clean of any hint of maturity and subtly altered with Dixon's cosmetics, peered back at me from the looking glass with an expression of youthful petulance that I scarcely recognised as my own.

"Remember," Dixon instructed as we made our final preparations, "you must inhabit your character completely. Observe how I maintain this slight tremor in my left hand, suggestive of a mild palsy. Such details lend authenticity to our performance."

As we departed Dixon's lodgings through a discreet rear entrance, I experienced the most peculiar sensation of having shed my very identity. In its place was a fiction of Dixon's creation, a schoolboy accompanying his grandmother to an exhibition of scientific curiosities. A perfect disguise, as he had promised, rendering us simultaneously visible and invisible—present yet beneath notice.

"Come along, Thomas," Dixon murmured, taking my arm with the proprietary familiarity of an elderly relative. "We have an appointment with the Mechanist."

Chapter 9
Alexandra Palace

The Palace of the People, as it has come to be known among Londoners, stood majestic upon its hill, commanding a view of the metropolis that stretched for miles in every direction. Since its reconstruction following the devastating conflagration of 1873, Alexandra Palace had already established itself as a monument to the recreational aspirations of the modern age. Its great glass domes, reminiscent of the Crystal Palace of Exhibition fame, glittered in the summer sunlight as Dixon and I approached along the tree-lined avenue.

Despite the warmth of the August afternoon, Dixon remained steadfast in his elaborate disguise, his gloved hand resting upon my arm with the tentative pressure appropriate to an elderly matron. The bombazine of his dress must have been intolerably hot, yet he betrayed not the slightest discomfort as we joined the throng of visitors ascending toward the Palace's grand entrance.

"Remember, Thomas," he murmured in that disconcertingly convincing falsetto he had adopted, "you are a reluctant companion to your grandmother's outing. Maintain an expression of adolescent ennui."

I slouched my shoulders dutifully and affected the petulant demeanour of a schoolboy deprived of more exciting diversions. My collar chafed abominably against my neck, and the wool of the blazer seemed specifically designed for maximum discomfort in summer weather.

The Palace grounds were thronged with visitors of every description. Nursemaids shepherded their excitable charges toward the helter-skelter and swing-boats, while gentlemen and their ladies promenaded along the formal gardens, parasols twirling above carefully arranged coiffures. A brass band played with martial enthusiasm from the bandstand, competing with the cacophonous strains of the steam carousel and the shouts of vendors hawking ices and ginger beer.

"We shall proceed as though merely perambulating the grounds," Dixon instructed, his eyes sharp beneath the shadow of his bonnet. "Make no obvious indication of our interest in any particular individual."

We had scarcely completed one circuit of the central fountain when Dixon's fingers tightened perceptibly upon my arm. Following the direction of his gaze, I observed a tall figure approaching from the direction of the north entrance, his identity unmistakable despite the press of the crowd.

The Mechanist cut a striking figure in his trademark Inverness cape of midnight black, the high collar partially obscuring a Venetian mask of polished silver that concealed the upper portion of his countenance. Beside him walked a military gentleman whose rigid posture and clipped moustache identified him instantly as General von Waldersee, resplendent in civilian attire of impeccable cut.

Most remarkable, however, were their companions—three identical Italian triplets, being of extraordinary height and breadth and moving with the synchronised precision of automata. These triplets formed a protective phalanx about the Mechanist and the General, their hawkish gaze sweeping the crowd with evident suspicion.

"How fortuitous," Dixon whispered. "Let us contrive to position ourselves advantageously."

With the practiced nonchalance of an elderly woman

seeking a moment's respite, Dixon guided us toward a nearby bench situated fortuitously within earshot of the path along which the Mechanist and his party were proceeding.

"Oh, Thomas," Dixon exclaimed in a carrying voice, "my poor old feet cannot bear another step. Be a good lad and allow your grandmother to rest a moment."

As we seated ourselves, the Mechanist and von Waldersee paused not ten yards distant, engaged in conversation of an evidently private nature. The Italian triplets arranged themselves in a defensive formation, effectively discouraging any approach from curious onlookers. Despite our proximity, their voices remained tantalizingly indistinct, the words carried away by the ambient clamour of the crowd and the persistent braying of the band.

"—cannot guarantee the efficacy without proper—" a fragment of the Mechanist's statement reached us, his accent bearing the unmistakable cadence of the Mediterranean.

The General's response was lost entirely, though his expression conveyed a gravity that belied the ostensibly festive surroundings.

To my astonishment, von Waldersee then produced a slender volume bound in what appeared to be red leather, which he presented to the Mechanist with evident ceremony. The latter received it with gloved hands, examining the tome with such intensity that I could perceive his satisfaction even through the expressionless mask.

"It is as you requested," the General's voice momentarily rose above the ambient noise.

Before further exchange could occur, one of the triplets leaned forward to murmur something in the Mechanist's ear. With a curt nod, the party proceeded toward a side entrance marked "Artistes Only", disappearing from view behind a nondescript door guarded by a uniformed attendant.

"Most illuminating," Dixon remarked, his voice resuming

its natural timbre momentarily before recollecting his disguise. "Though I confess I had hoped for more substantive intelligence."

Scarce ten minutes had elapsed when a ripple of excitement passed through the crowd assembled near the east entrance. A curious conveyance approached along the carriage way—a cycle rickshaw of decidedly Oriental design, powered by a bare-chested Hindu of impressive musculature. Seated upon the cushioned bench of this exotic vehicle was a figure whose appearance elicited gasps of recognition from numerous female spectators.

Swami Saraswati, for it could be none other, presented a vision of Eastern mysticism calculated to entrance the Western imagination. His beard, black as a raven's wing, descended to his waist, while his golden robes caught the sunlight with an almost supernatural radiance. Upon his brow, a circular marking of vermilion stood out against his copper skin like a third eye of legend.

As the rickshaw halted at the foot of the marble steps, a veritable swarm of fashionable ladies converged upon the Swami, many dropping to their knees upon the gravel with scant regard for their expensive gowns. The Swami descended with regal deliberation, his hands raised in benediction.

"Blessings of the Divine Mother upon you, my children," his melodious voice carried across the hushed assembly. "May the cosmic harmony flow through your spirits."

With practiced benevolence, he moved among his devotees, bestowing a touch here, a murmured word there, each recipient transfigured with evident rapture. After completing this impromptu ceremony, the Swami and his entourage likewise proceeded toward the performers' entrance, where they were admitted without challenge.

"Come, Thomas," Dixon announced, rising with the careful movements of advanced age. "We must secure advantageous positions for the performance."

As we made our way toward the great auditorium, I could not suppress a frisson of apprehension. What connection bound these disparate figures—a German military man, an enigmatic mechanical showman, and an Eastern spiritual leader—in common purpose? The book that had passed between them seemed to hold some significance beyond its modest appearance.

The vast hall was already filling rapidly as we entered, the excited murmur of anticipation rising to the vaulted ceiling. Dixon guided us with unerring precision toward seats in the middle distance, neither too prominent nor too remote from the stage.

"Observe everything," he instructed beneath his breath. "The slightest detail may prove consequential."

The great crystal chandeliers began to dim, plunging the auditorium into expectant darkness. A single spotlight illuminated the crimson curtain, behind which waited the Mechanist and whatever marvels—or horrors—he had prepared for the entertainment of London society.

Chapter 10
The Trance

The auditorium fell into an expectant hush as the last of the crystal chandeliers dimmed, plunging the assembled throng into momentary darkness. A single arc light sprang to life, its harsh white beam piercing the gloom to illuminate a solitary figure upon the stage.

Swami Saraswati stood motionless, his golden robes catching the light with an almost supernatural radiance. His arms were raised in benediction, the voluminous sleeves falling away to reveal limbs of surprising muscularity for one ostensibly devoted to spiritual rather than physical pursuits.

"Beloved children of the Divine Mother," his mellifluous voice caressed the audience, carrying to the furthest reaches of the hall without apparent effort. "It is with profound joy that I present to you my most beloved friend from Italia, the incomparable Mechanist."

A murmur of anticipation rippled through the crowd. Beside me, Dixon leaned forward imperceptibly in his disguise as an elderly matron, his keen eyes fixed upon the stage.

"He is not merely a practitioner of scientific wonders," continued the Swami, his hands describing elaborate patterns in the air, "but a great sage and warrior of love, whose mission is to unite humanity in cosmic harmony."

The Swami closed his eyes, his body swaying slightly as though moved by invisible currents. "I bestow the blessings of Brahma, Vishnu, and Shiva upon this assembly. May the universal consciousness flow through your mortal vessels."

The spotlight widened, revealing a trapdoor in the center of the stage from which a platform now rose with theatrical deliberation. Upon it stood the Mechanist, resplendent in his trademark Inverness cape, his silver Venetian mask gleaming beneath the harsh illumination. Beside him, a vision in scarlet silk, stood a statuesque blonde woman whose extraordinary height was further accentuated by the most precarious stiletto heels I had ever beheld.

"The assistant from The George," I whispered to Dixon, an involuntary shudder passing through my frame as I recalled our previous encounter with the female in question. The mysterious woman had, through some scientific means I could neither comprehend nor explain, succeeded in igniting my hair from a distance of no less than ten feet.

"Indeed," murmured Dixon, his voice a barely audible whisper beneath the enthusiastic applause that greeted the Mechanist's appearance.

The masked figure stepped forward, his gloved hands spread in a gesture of invitation. "Ladies and gentlemen," his accent caressed each syllable with Mediterranean flair, "for my first demonstration, I require the assistance of a volunteer from the audience. A lady of mature years would be most suitable."

Before anyone else could respond, Dixon rose to his feet with surprising alacrity for one supposedly burdened with the infirmities of age.

"I should be delighted to assist, kind sir," he called in his faltering feminine voice, already making his way toward the aisle with the hesitant gait of the elderly.

I watched with mingled admiration and trepidation as Dixon ascended the steps to the stage, playing the role of a fluttered elderly matron to perfection. The Mechanist received him with exaggerated gallantry, bowing over Dixon's gloved hand.

"Your name, madame?"

"Mrs. Edith Clarence, sir," Dixon replied with a simpering smile that transformed his disguised features into a mask as effective as the Mechanist's own.

"Mrs. Clarence," the Mechanist repeated, his voice carrying throughout the hall, "I shall now induce in you a state of hypnotic trance, during which you shall discover capabilities beyond your ordinary experience."

What followed was a display of conventional mesmeric technique, the Mechanist employing the standard passes and incantations familiar to any habitué of the music hall. Dixon, playing his role with consummate skill, allowed his eyelids to flutter closed, his body swaying in apparent response to the Mechanist's ministrations.

The blonde assistant brought forward two straight-backed chairs, positioning them some six feet apart upon the stage. The Mechanist continued his hypnotic patter, his right hand touching Dixon's arms, shoulders, and finally his forehead.

"Rigid and stiff as a rock," he intoned, his voice dropping to a resonant baritone. "Rigid and stiff as a rock. Every muscle, every sinew, transformed to unyielding stone."

He repeated the phrase several times, each repetition accompanied by a delicate touch to Dixon's body. To my astonishment, Dixon's form seemed to grow increasingly rigid, his limbs assuming an unnatural stillness.

With a dramatic flourish, the Mechanist pressed his palm against Dixon's shoulder, causing him to topple backward like a felled tree. The assistant moved with extraordinary swiftness, catching Dixon's head before it could strike the stage. Together, they maneuvered Dixon's rigid form until he was suspended horizontally between the two chairs, his head supported by one, his ankles by the other, with nothing beneath his torso.

A drum roll emanated from the orchestral pit, heightening the dramatic tension. From the wings emerged the Italian triplets we had observed earlier, their identical features rendered more striking by the theatrical lighting. Clad in form-fitting costumes of silver and black, they moved with the synchronised precision I had noted during our earlier observation.

The triplets began to circle the suspended Dixon, their movements evolving from a deliberate processional pace into an increasingly elaborate choreography. The audience gasped as one of the triplets suddenly vaulted onto Dixon's midsection, standing upon his abdomen as though it were a platform of solid marble.

A second triplet followed, climbing onto the shoulders of the first with acrobatic grace. The third, grasping a silken rope that descended from the rafters, was drawn swiftly upward before descending to perch atop the human pyramid, three men balanced upon the seemingly petrified form of an elderly woman.

The audience erupted in thunderous applause. The triplets continued their balancing act, standing upon Dixon's still-rigid form as the Mechanist approached them.

"Mrs. Clarence," he addressed his subject, "how do you feel?"

To my astonishment, Dixon replied in his falsetto voice, without the slightest indication of strain, "I am feeling quite well, thank you, though I remain somewhat concerned about Lord Salisbury's resignation."

This topical political reference elicited appreciative chuckles from the more well-informed members of the audience.

The triplets dismounted with balletic precision. Having completed their bow, they grasped their silken ropes once more and ascended with simian agility, disappearing among the decorative swags and pendants suspended from the ceiling.

The Mechanist assisted Dixon to his feet, and the latter

made his way back to our seats with the slightly disoriented air appropriate to one emerging from hypnotic suggestion. No sooner had he resumed his place beside me than a voice called out from several rows behind us.

"I say, sir," a corpulent gentleman of middle years addressed the Mechanist, "might you be persuaded to make me 'rigid and stiff' as well? My wife has been requesting such a service for quite some time."

A wave of ribald laughter rolled through the auditorium. The Mechanist acknowledged the jest with a courtly bow, but was prevented from responding by the return of Swami Saraswati to the stage.

"Beloved ones," the Swami proclaimed, his arms outstretched, "my brother the Mechanist has come bearing a message of universal love that transcends the boundaries of creed and nation."

The Mechanist stepped forward to join the Swami at center stage. Their hands clasped in fraternal greeting, they began to circle one another in a stately pavane, their movements gradually accelerating into a whirling dervish-like rotation.

A curious transformation came over the audience as this peculiar dance continued. Initially subtle—a swaying here, a humming there—it rapidly developed into a most extraordinary display of spontaneous behaviour. Ladies and gentlemen alike rose from their seats, embracing strangers with uninhibited fervour. Guttural moans and ecstatic cries filled the air as members of the audience began to dance in the aisles, their movements lacking all semblance of conventional propriety.

"Swami! Swami! Swami!" The chant began softly but swelled with frightening rapidity into a deafening chorus. To my horror, several gentlemen of otherwise respectable appearance began to clamber onto the stage, followed by ladies who showed no regard for the preservation of their modesty as they hitched their skirts to join the growing throng.

The triplets reappeared, attempting to form a cordon between the performers and the encroaching audience members. The blonde assistant joined their efforts, her remarkable strength evident as she physically restrained several would-be invaders. Their efforts proved futile, however, as the sheer numbers of the entranced audience members overwhelmed their defensive line.

Suddenly, a cacophony of feline yowls pierced through the din of the crowd. From every corner of the auditorium, cats of all descriptions came streaming in—sleek black ones with gleaming yellow eyes, calicos with patches of orange and white, tabby cats with striped patterns, even pampered Persians still wearing their jeweled collars. They poured through doors, leapt from balconies, and squeezed through impossibly narrow openings, their collective meowing reaching a crescendo that rivaled the human commotion.

The cats moved with singular purpose, weaving between the legs of the entranced audience members, causing several to stumble and fall. Some leapt directly onto the backs of the encroaching crowd, their claws extended, while others darted toward the stage with alarming speed and precision. A particularly massive tomcat with battle-scarred ears led the charge, his tail held high like a standard-bearer leading troops into battle.

"Good God!" I exclaimed, watching as a stream of tabbies flowed past my feet like a living river. "It's happening again—just like at Stepney Green!"

The triplets, already overwhelmed by the human onslaught, now faced a furry insurrection from below. One of them staggered backward as a half-dozen cats swarmed up his legs and torso, climbing him as though he were a tree. The blonde assistant kicked off several cats that had attached themselves to her scarlet skirts, but for every one she dislodged, three more took their place.

The Mechanist, visibly alarmed by this unexpected development, shouted something to the Swami in a language I couldn't identify. The Swami's normally serene expression faltered as he stared at the sea of cats now converging on the stage, their eyes reflecting the stage lights with an eerie, luminous quality.

A Persian with luxurious white fur leapt directly onto the Mechanist's control panel, batting at the dials and levers with curious paws. Sparks flew as its tail swept across an exposed wire, eliciting a sharp electrical crack and a pained yowl from the unfortunate creature.

Dixon grabbed my arm, his eyes alight with realisation. "The cats, Paul! They're responding to the same frequency as the humans, but with the opposite effect. Instead of entrancement, they're experiencing agitation. Extraordinary!"

The scene had descended into absolute chaos—humans pushing forward in ecstatic fervour, cats streaming in with single-minded determination, and the performers retreating in evident panic as their careful orchestration collapsed around them in a symphony of meows, shouts, and the continuous electrical hum of the Mechanist's disrupted equipment.

The Mechanist and the Swami retreated hastily toward the wings, pursued by a veritable mob of ecstatic devotees.

Dixon grasped my arm with surprising strength. "Quickly, Paul," he hissed, abandoning his feminine disguise in the urgency of the moment. "The Artistes' Entrance. We must intercept them."

We extricated ourselves from the pandemonium with some difficulty, Dixon leading me through a labyrinthine series of corridors with unerring certainty, suggesting a familiarity with the Palace's architecture that he had not previously disclosed.

"Here," he whispered, pulling me into the shadow of a decorative column adjacent to a door marked "Artistes Only".

"They must emerge at this point if they wish to reach their conveyances."

Scarce had we taken up our position when the door burst open. The Mechanist emerged at a near run, clutching a book to his chest—the same volume, I was certain, that General von Waldersee had presented to him earlier. The Swami followed close behind, his formerly serene countenance distorted with evident alarm.

Before I could comprehend his intention, Dixon launched himself from our hiding place with the agility of a man half his age. He collided with the Mechanist in what appeared to be an embrace of passionate intensity, his arms encircling the caped figure as he attempted—to my utter astonishment—to press his lips against the silver mask.

The Mechanist recoiled with a cry of revulsion, shoving Dixon aside with such force that my companion was propelled against the opposite wall. Without a backward glance, the Mechanist and Swami continued their headlong flight toward the carriage drive, where I glimpsed a waiting brougham with the Italian triplets already mounted on the exterior.

I rushed to Dixon's assistance, helping him to regain his feet. His bonnet had been dislodged in the scuffle, revealing his own features beneath the theatrical cosmetics.

"Dixon! Are you injured?" I inquired, genuinely concerned by the violence of his collision with the wall.

To my bewilderment, his expression was one of triumph rather than pain. From beneath his shawl, he produced a slender volume bound in red leather.

"Behold, Paul," he declared with evident satisfaction, "the object of our expedition."

I stared in disbelief at the book in his hands, its gilt title clearly legible against the crimson binding: "Vom Kriege," by Carl von Clausewitz.

"On War?" I translated aloud, my classical education serving to render the German title into English. "The Prussian treatise on military strategy?"

"The very same," Dixon confirmed, straightening his disheveled disguise with the practiced movements of one accustomed to rapid transformations. "Though I suspect this particular copy contains annotations of a nature far removed from conventional military doctrine."

As we made our way toward the exit, the sounds of continued chaos echoed from the auditorium behind us. I found myself trembling, not merely from the excitement of our adventure, but from a profound disquiet regarding the events we had witnessed.

"Dixon," I ventured, "what manner of influence did the Mechanist and the Swami exert over that audience? It was as though some form of mass hysteria had been deliberately induced."

Dixon's expression darkened. "Indeed, Paul. And if such influence can be wielded within the confines of Alexandra Palace, one must consider the implications were it to be deployed in contexts of greater consequence."

The red volume in his hand seemed to pulse with ominous significance as we emerged into the gathering dusk of the summer evening.

Chapter 11
The Antenna

We stood in the gathering twilight, watching as the brougham bearing the Mechanist and his entourage disappeared down the long drive of Alexandra Palace, pursued by a most extraordinary cavalcade of entranced devotees. Ladies with their coiffures in disarray and gentlemen missing hats, ties, and in some cases even shoes, continued their relentless pursuit long after any hope of catching the swift carriage had been extinguished. Curiously, the procession was preceded by a large group of cats, growing larger by the minute, as new felines joined their ranks from all directions.

"Most peculiar behaviour," I remarked, adjusting my school cap, which had become somewhat askew during our recent adventure.

Dixon, who had hastily rearranged his bonnet and shawl to restore his elderly female disguise, made no immediate reply. His gaze was fixed not upon the departing revelers but upon the Palace itself, his eyes narrowed in concentration.

"Come, Thomas," he instructed, resuming his faltering falsetto. "Your grandmother requires a constitutional before our homeward journey."

Thus we began a curious perambulation of the Palace grounds, Dixon setting a pace remarkably brisk for one ostensibly burdened with the infirmities of advanced age. We proceeded along paths less frequented by the general public,

Dixon periodically pausing to scrutinise some architectural feature or ornamental shrubbery with intense interest.

"May I inquire as to the object of our search?" I ventured after we had completed perhaps three-quarters of our circuit.

"Patience, dear boy," Dixon replied, his affected voice dropping momentarily to its natural register. "When one seeks to influence the minds of hundreds simultaneously, certain scientific apparatus becomes necessary. Such apparatus requires..." He hesitated, scanning the roofline of the eastern wing. "Ah! There!"

Following the direction of his gaze, I observed nothing of immediate significance—merely an ornamental finial atop a decorative turret. Dixon, however, increased our pace, guiding us toward a maintenance path that led behind the east wing.

As we rounded the corner of the building, the path opened onto a small clearing ordinarily inaccessible to the public. What I beheld there caused me to halt in mid-stride, a gasp of astonishment escaping my lips before I could suppress it.

Rising from the center of the clearing was a metallic structure of the most extraordinary design. A central mast of gleaming copper ascended perhaps twenty feet into the air, surmounted by a complex arrangement of wires and rods forming a geometrical pattern reminiscent of an inverted umbrella. At the terminus of each rod, a spherical object of some crystalline substance caught the last rays of the setting sun, refracting them into prismatic beams.

Beneath this curious edifice, illuminated by the harsh glare of electric arc lamps, General von Waldersee himself directed the activities of four assistants clad in the unmistakable field gray of the Prussian military, though they wore no insignia of rank or regiment. With practiced efficiency, they were dismantling various components of electrical equipment, stowing them in large wooden crates stenciled with what appeared to be technical designations in German script.

The General supervised their efforts with the critical eye of one accustomed to command, occasionally barking instructions in guttural Teutonic phrases. A portable steam generator hissed and throbbed nearby, powering the electric lamps and, I presumed, whatever function the antenna had recently served.

So intent were we upon this unexpected tableau that we failed to maintain adequate concealment. One of the German assistants glanced in our direction, his eyes widening with alarm. He spoke urgently to von Waldersee, who straightened from his inspection of a brass apparatus to fix us with a penetrating stare.

"Halt! Wer ist da?" he called, his hand moving instinctively to his side where, in military attire, a sidearm would normally reside.

Dixon, without the slightest hesitation, adopted an expression of befuddled elderly confusion. "Oh my goodness," he exclaimed in his quavering soprano, "I do believe we have taken a wrong turning, Thomas. How very careless of us."

The General advanced toward us, his assistants moving to flank him in a manner suggesting training beyond that of mere technicians. As they drew closer, I observed that their hands bore the distinctive calluses and powder burns characteristic of artillery specialists rather than laboratory assistants.

"This area is verboten—forbidden—to the public," von Waldersee stated, his English precise but heavily accented. "You will depart immediately."

Dixon adopted an expression of flustered apology. "Oh dear, how terribly embarrassing. We were merely seeking a vantage point from which my grandson might observe the fireworks display. The boy has a passionate interest in pyrotechnics, you see."

The General's gaze shifted to me, his eyes cold as the waters of the Baltic. "You should take your grandson elsewhere to play, grandmother, and stop invading private property."

"How fascinating," Dixon replied, his tone suggesting the mild interest of an elderly woman with no comprehension of scientific affairs. "Do come along, Thomas. We mustn't disturb these gentlemen further."

I allowed Dixon to lead me away, maintaining the sullen demeanour of an adolescent deprived of an anticipated entertainment. As we rounded the corner of the building, safely out of earshot, Dixon's grip on my arm tightened fractionally.

"Just as I suspected," he murmured, his natural voice returning. "The Mechanist's performance was mere theatrical distraction. The true purpose lay in that apparatus."

"What manner of device was that?" I inquired, glancing back toward the clearing with renewed unease.

"A transmitting antenna of most sophisticated design," Dixon replied, his pace increasing as we made our way toward the main avenue. "Designed to broadcast electrical impulses at a specific frequency. When combined with certain chemical compounds and psychological techniques, such impulses can influence the electrical activity of the human brain."

"You suggest that the audience's extraordinary behaviour was induced by that machine?" The implications were so disturbing that I found myself resisting the conclusion despite the evidence of my own senses.

"Precisely." Dixon nodded. "The Mechanist's theatrical spectacle, the Swami's supposed spiritual influence—these were merely delivery mechanisms for a more scientific form of control. The true experiment was not upon the stage but throughout the auditorium."

We had reached the main carriage drive, where hansom cabs and private conveyances still waited to collect those audience members who had not joined the frenzied pursuit of the Mechanist's brougham. Dixon hailed a cab with the imperious confidence of a gentleman rather than the diffidence of an elderly matron, momentarily forgetting his disguise in his scientific excitement.

As we settled into the relative privacy of the hansom, I ventured the question that had been troubling me since our departure from the clearing. "But what could be the purpose of such an experiment? Surely not a mere theatrical sensation?"

Dixon's expression darkened as he removed his bonnet, wiping the theatrical cosmetics from his face with a handkerchief. "Consider, Paul, the strategic implications of a technology that could render an assembly of individuals insensible to reason, susceptible to suggestion, and moved by powerful emotional impulses not their own."

"A terrible weapon," I murmured, the full import of his words dawning upon me.

"Indeed. And with the assistance of General von Waldersee, formerly Chief of the German General Staff, such a weapon might find application far beyond the harmless confines of a music hall entertainment." Dixon patted the pocket containing Clausewitz's treatise. "The conjunction of Prussian military doctrine with this new technology presents possibilities I scarcely dare contemplate."

As our cab rattled through the darkening streets toward London proper, I found myself haunted by the image of that gleaming antenna, its crystalline spheres capturing and transforming the light of the setting sun—just as the minds of the audience had been captured and transformed by whatever invisible forces it had projected into their midst.

Chapter 12
A Riddle

The morning found us at The Gun, that venerable establishment in the Docklands where Dixon maintained a curious acquaintance with the landlord, a former naval gunner of formidable aspect and equally formidable discretion. Despite the early hour, the taproom was already occupied by a scattering of stevedores and lightermen breaking their fast before the commencement of their labours.

We had abandoned our disguises, Dixon having determined that the theatrical cosmetics would attract more attention than they would deflect in the honest surroundings of a dockside tavern. I confess I welcomed the return to my customary attire, the school uniform having chafed in places best left unmentioned.

Dixon spread the morning newspapers across our table with a theatrical flourish. "Observe, Paul," he directed, tapping a headline with his forefinger. "The consequences of our scientific friends' exhibition."

I leaned forward to read the alarming report:

VIOLENT DISORDER FOLLOWS EXHIBITION AT ALEXANDRA PALACE Police Battle Frenzied Crowds in Wood Green and Muswell Hill

"Good heavens," I murmured, scanning the account. "It states that following the performance, hundreds of spectators pursued the performers' carriage through the streets, their numbers growing as they progressed. By nightfall, the throng had transformed into a mob of riotous character, demanding access to what they termed 'the Mechanist's blessing'."

Dixon nodded grimly. "Read on."

"The disturbances spread throughout Wood Green, with particular concentration in Muswell Hill and Crouch Hill," I continued. "Numerous businesses suffered damage as the crowd attempted to locate the whereabouts of the performers. Police reinforcements were summoned from four divisions, yet the disorder persisted until the early hours of the morning."

"Most interesting," Dixon remarked, sipping his coffee with the air of a naturalist observing the predictable behaviour of a specimen. "The effects of the antenna persisted well beyond the initial exposure."

"You suggest the rioters remained under some form of influence?"

"Precisely. The electromagnetic impulses appear to have induced a persistent alteration of mental state. Most concerning."

Our discourse was interrupted by the approach of a young woman bearing a tray with our breakfast. Alice favoured me with a smile that brought an involuntary warmth to my countenance.

"Good morning, Mr. White," she greeted me, her voice carrying the melodious cadence of her native Cornwall. "Mr. Dixon. Your kippers and toast."

As she arranged our plates with practiced efficiency, I found myself momentarily distracted by the graceful movements of her hands. Dixon's knowing glance suggested my admiration had not gone unnoticed, but he was gentleman enough to refrain from comment.

"Oh, Mr. Dixon," Alice added as she straightened, "a gentleman left this for you yesterday evening. Most insistent it should be delivered into your hands personally." From her apron pocket she produced a sealed envelope of good-quality vellum.

"Did this gentleman provide a name?" Dixon inquired, examining the envelope with professional suspicion.

"He did not, sir. Tall gentleman, foreign-like in his speech." She hesitated. "There was something peculiar about him, if you don't mind my saying so. The way he moved... almost as if he wasn't accustomed to his own limbs."

Dixon's eyebrows rose fractionally at this observation. "Thank you, Alice. Your powers of perception do you credit."

She acknowledged the compliment with a modest nod before returning to her duties behind the bar, though not without a parting glance in my direction that sent my pulse racing in a most unprofessional manner.

Dixon waited until she was beyond earshot before breaking the seal of the envelope. He withdrew a single sheet of paper covered in an elegant copperplate hand.

"Most intriguing," he murmured, passing the letter to me after a cursory examination. I read aloud, keeping my voice low enough to avoid being overheard by our fellow patrons:

In this game of cat and mouse
There's a gate that named a house.
Chronos sits there on the wall,
Numbers, poems in his thrall.
We shall meet with you at Tea,
At the twelve, one, two, and three,
At the eight, seven, six, five, four,
Come alone to the tavern's door.
On the day our Lord arose,
You and I will wear a rose.
DM

"DM," Dixon repeated thoughtfully. "Dominico, perhaps? The apprentice of Bertini, whom we suspect may be our

Mechanist."

"Or perhaps," I ventured, recalling my schoolboy Latin, "'Don Mechanist'—Mr. Mechanist in Italian parlance."

Dixon nodded, conceding the possibility. "Now to the substance of the riddle itself." He retrieved the letter, studying it with narrowed eyes. "The writer proposes a meeting, that much is evident. But the location is concealed within this poetic cipher."

"'There's a gate that named a house,'" I quoted. "That suggests a location in London where a gate gave its name to a building or residence."

"Several possibilities present themselves," Dixon mused. "The Gatehouse at Westminster, Queen's Gate in Kensington, Highgate to the north... And, of course, one of the historic seven gates of the London Wall—Newgate." The expression on Dixon's face changed momentarily.

"Aldgate, Bishopsgate, Moorgate," I continued, mentally cataloguing London's historic entrances as much to distract Dixon (and myself) from the memories of Newgate as to solve the riddle.

"Ludgate," Dixon added with particular emphasis. "From the old Saxon king Lud, who was said to be buried there. And indeed, there is Ludgate House, upon which sits a famous clock."

His eyes brightened with the excitement of intellectual pursuit. "And there we have our Chronos—the personification of time in Greek mythology. The clock on Ludgate House has the twelve letters L-U-D-G-A-T-E-H-O-U-S-E in place of the numerals."

I saw the connection immediately. "So the sequence 'twelve, one, two, and three, at the eight, seven, six, five, four' corresponds to particular letters!"

Dixon was already scribbling on the margin of the newspaper, mapping the numbers to their corresponding letters.

"Twelve is L, one is U, two is D, three is G..." His pencil moved rapidly. "Eight is H, seven is O, six is U, five is S, four is E."

"G-A-T-E-H-O-U-S-E," I read over his shoulder. "That's not quite right. It should spell Ludgate House."

"Not if we're selecting letters," Dixon corrected.

"I see," I agreed.

"Indeed. And where might one find a notorious Gate House?"

I racked my brain for the connection. "Highgate," I realised suddenly. "The Gate House Tavern in Highgate Village!"

Dixon nodded approvingly. "Precisely. Now, the time of our proposed rendezvous is indicated by 'Tea'."

"The letter T appears in Ludgate House at position..." I mentally counted. "The twentieth letter of the alphabet, so—"

"No, no," Dixon interrupted. "More straightforward than that. T is the third letter in the sequence L-U-D-G-A-T-E. The clock position would be two o'clock."

"But the verse specifically mentions 'Tea'," I insisted. "Not merely the letter T. In society parlance, afternoon tea is traditionally served at four o'clock."

Dixon reconsidered, his fingers drumming thoughtfully on the table. "You may have the right of it. 'Tea' could indeed indicate the social hour rather than the alphabetical position. But why would it be capitalised?"

"And 'the day our Lord arose' is clearly Sunday," I added. "With roses as our means of mutual identification."

"This coming Sunday, then," Dixon concluded. "The Gate House Tavern at Highgate, two o'clock. We shall arrive early to reconnoiter the surroundings."

"We?" I questioned. "The letter specifically instructs you to 'come alone to the tavern's door'."

Dixon dismissed this with a wave of his hand. "A standard precaution in clandestine meetings. One which I have no intention of honouring. The Mechanist has already demonstrated capabilities beyond the conventional; I shall not confront such an adversary without reliable support."

"Dixon, the peril—" I began, but he silenced me with a sharp gesture.

"The matter is decided, Paul. You shall accompany me to Highgate on Sunday next, though you will maintain a discreet distance during the initial contact."

His tone brooked no argument, yet I could not suppress a sense of foreboding at the prospect of this rendezvous with our mysterious correspondent. As I raised my teacup to conceal my disquiet, I caught sight of Alice behind the bar. Her gaze met mine, her expression suggesting she had observed more of our intense conversation than I might have wished. There was concern in her eyes—concern, I realised with a mixture of pleasure and apprehension, that was directed specifically toward my person.

Dixon, following the direction of my gaze, permitted himself a rare smile. "It appears, my dear Paul, that our investigation has attracted interest from quarters beyond the scientific community."

I felt the warmth of embarrassment suffuse my features. "I'm sure I don't know what you mean," I replied with as much dignity as I could muster.

"Of course not," Dixon agreed, his voice laden with gentlemanly amusement. "Now, shall we return to the matter of our mysterious correspondent? I believe there may be additional significance to the choice of Highgate as our meeting place..."

Chapter 13
A Confrontation

Sunday afternoon found Dixon and me approaching Highgate Village by separate routes, a precaution he had insisted upon despite my protestations. The day was pleasant enough, the early June sunshine casting dappled shadows through the leaves of the *Platanus x hispanica* trees lining Highgate Hill. I had secured a single red rose to my lapel as instructed, though the flower felt more like a target than a means of identification.

Dixon had proceeded ahead, instructing me to enter The Gate House precisely seven minutes after his own arrival—sufficient time, he explained, for him to assess the environment without the appearance of companions. I observed him from a discreet distance as he ascended the steps to the tavern's entrance, the rose in his buttonhole a crimson splash against his somber attire.

After consulting my pocket watch with perhaps greater frequency than necessary, I followed, pushing open the heavy oak door to find myself in the tavern's main saloon. The interior was cool and dim after the brightness of the afternoon, the air redolent with the comforting aromas of beer and tobacco. Several patrons occupied tables near the windows, enjoying their Sunday refreshments with the measured tranquility appropriate to the Sabbath.

Dixon was nowhere to be seen, though the barman caught my eye with a knowing nod toward the staircase leading to the upper rooms.

Inside, the Gate House revealed itself as a warren of interconnected rooms, each with its own distinct character, while maintaining the essential qualities of a traditional English public house. The main saloon, immediately to the right of the entrance, was the largest of these spaces. Its ceiling was low, crossed by heavy oak beams blackened by centuries of tobacco smoke before recent regulations curtailed such practices. The walls were panelled in dark wood to waist height, above which hung an eclectic collection of framed engravings, local maps, and memorabilia chronicling Highgate's evolution from rural hamlet to prosperous suburb. The floor was of wide, uneven planks that creaked reassuringly underfoot, telling tales of countless patrons who had crossed their surface over generations.

To the left of the main saloon was what was once designated as the "Ladies' Parlour"—a smaller, more intimate room where genteel female patrons might take refreshment without enduring the occasionally boisterous atmosphere of the main bar. This space had retained its more refined character, with comfortable upholstered settees arranged around small tables, and wallpaper of a subtly floral pattern replacing the wooden panelling found elsewhere.

A narrow passage led to the rear of the establishment, where a surprisingly spacious dining room accommodated those seeking more substantial fare than the cold cuts and savory pies offered at the bar. Here, the ceiling rose higher, and windows on three sides admitted ample natural light during daylight hours. The floorboards were partially covered by a faded Turkish carpet of complex pattern, its colours muted by years of service but still lending warmth to the space.

The upper floors of the Gate House, reached by a narrow staircase near the back passage, comprised several private dining rooms and meeting chambers of varying sizes. These were often engaged by local societies and gentlemen's clubs for their regular gatherings, particularly the large room that occupied most of the second floor front. This impressive chamber featured a vaulted ceiling, substantial windows overlooking the High Street, and walls adorned with portraits of notable Highgate residents from centuries past.

Beyond its physical attributes, the Gate House served as something of a temporal anchor for Highgate Village. It had witnessed the transformation of the area from a rural outpost favoured by wealthy Londoners seeking cleaner air to a fully integrated suburb with its own distinct identity and traditions. The tavern had played host to literary figures including Coleridge and Dickens, provided refreshment to weary travellers making their way northward from the capital, and served as an unofficial community centre for generations of local residents.

I ventured upstairs, where the small bar was nearly empty, and approached the counter, intending to purchase a drink as a pretext for my presence.

"A pale ale, if you please," I requested, affecting the casual air of a man with no purpose beyond slaking his thirst.

As the barman drew my drink, I felt the sudden pressure of a hand upon my shoulder—a firm grip, not hostile but insistent. I turned, expecting perhaps a chance encounter with some acquaintance, only to find myself staring into the unmasked countenance of the Mechanist.

Without his silver Venetian disguise, he presented a visage I found disturbingly familiar, though I could not immediately place where I might have encountered him before. His features were distinctly Mediterranean—olive complexion, prominent nose, dark eyes beneath heavy brows—yet there was something in their arrangement that suggested recognition.

"Signor White," he addressed me, his Italian accent less pronounced than during his theatrical performances, but unmistakably present. "Would you be so kind as to call your friend Signor Dixon? I am aware that you arrived together, despite instructions to the contrary."

His tone was conversational, even cordial, yet carried an undercurrent of authority that brooked no refusal. I glanced instinctively toward the staircase.

"He awaits you above," the Mechanist confirmed with a smile that did not reach his eyes. "Shall we join him? We have matters of mutual interest to discuss."

With no graceful means of refusal, I followed him up the narrow staircase to the tavern's upper room. This space, clearly reserved for private gatherings, contained several tables arranged beneath exposed oak beams. The chamber was nearly empty save for Dixon, who occupied a table in the far corner, his back to the wall in a position that afforded him clear view of both the staircase and the windows.

"Ah, Paul," Dixon greeted me with practiced nonchalance. "I see you have made the acquaintance of our correspondent."

The Mechanist gestured for me to take the seat beside Dixon, while he positioned himself across the table. No introductions were exchanged; none were necessary. The three of us regarded one another in momentary silence, like chess masters assessing the board before the opening gambit.

Dixon broke the impasse. "You requested this meeting, sir. May I inquire as to its purpose?"

The Mechanist leaned forward, his elbows upon the table, fingers steepled in a gesture reminiscent of Dixon's own habitual pose. "I am aware, Signor Dixon, that you possess an *articolo* of considerable scientific and historical significance—the personal diary of Countess Ada Lovelace."

Dixon's expression remained impassive. "And if such an item were in my possession?"

"I am prepared to offer a most handsome sum for its acquisition," the Mechanist replied. "Let us say, ten thousand pounds sterling."

Throughout this exchange, I found myself repeatedly distracted by the Mechanist's countenance, struggling to place the elusive familiarity it evoked. Something in the set of his jaw, perhaps, or the particular angle at which he held his head...

Dixon's response was cool and measured. "Even if I possessed such an item, sir, I would not consider transferring it to one who has demonstrated such willingness to abuse scientific principles for personal aggrandisement."

The Mechanist's lips curved in a smile of genuine amusement. "Come now, Signor Dixon. We are men of the world. Every scientist who has ever lived has, in some measure, 'abused' his knowledge for personal gain. Newton used his position at the Royal Mint to persecute counterfeiters. Galileo curried favour with the Medici. Even your revered Faraday performed parlour tricks for the amusement of London society."

He leaned back in his chair, regarding us with the indulgent air of a schoolmaster addressing promising but naive pupils. "My feelings toward Britain are not those of disdain, but rather of amusement. Your parliamentary system—so proud you are of it!—grants influence to the weak-minded and power to the stupid. A butcher from Whitechapel may cast a vote with the same weight as a Fellow of the Royal Society."

"And who, in your estimation, should wield power?" Dixon inquired, his tone one of academic interest rather than moral outrage.

"Rome," the Mechanist replied without hesitation.

"By which you mean yourself," Dixon corrected.

The Mechanist inclined his head in acknowledgement. "At least I possess the intellectual honesty to admit as much. Your British *ipocrisia*—pretending that power should reside with the commonality while your aristocracy pulls the strings from behind their curtains of tradition—it offends reason itself."

"An interesting philosophical position," Dixon observed. "However, it does not alter my response regarding the Lovelace diary. You shall have it only over my dead body."

"That," the Mechanist replied with chilling equanimity, "can be arranged."

"I wouldn't try it, if I were you."

"Rest assured that if you attempt to bring destruction down upon me, I shall do the same to you, Signor Dixon."

My attention, which had been divided between the conversation and my persistent attempt to place the Mechanist's face, was abruptly focused by a slight movement beneath the table. The Mechanist's hands, which had disappeared from view during our discourse, now held two small pistols—Belgian-made Bulldog revolvers, if I was not mistaken—their barrels directed with disturbing precision at the region of our respective generative organs under the bar table.

"Please maintain your *compostezza*, gentlemen," the Mechanist instructed, his voice now entirely devoid of its previous conviviality. "A single bullet at this range would ensure that neither of you would leave descendants to mourn your passing."

Dixon remained unnaturally still, though I detected a tensing of his jaw that suggested calculation rather than fear.

"You know," the Mechanist continued, his voice animated by a sudden fervour, "what gives me the greatest pleasure in my performances? Not the applause, not the financial reward, but the programming of people—these mindless automata who ridiculously believe themselves possessed of free will. These stupid men... *Questi uomini stupidi, questi stupidi inferiori, donne, neri, indiani, ebrei, arabi, immigrati...*"

"Where does it stop?" asked Dixon. "And do you genuinely believe that it stops at you?"

The Mechanist gave no reply. His eyes gleamed with a zealot's intensity. "With the correct sequence of stimuli—

visual cues, verbal suggestions, electromagnetic frequencies—the human brain becomes as *malleabile*... as *cera*... wax. I have made respectable matrons disrobe in public, caused bankers to empty their pockets into the hands of beggars, transformed pacifists into berserkers with a single phrase."

As his tirade grew more impassioned, I observed a subtle movement behind him—a shadow detaching itself from the dimness near the staircase. The Mechanist, engrossed in his monologue, remained oblivious.

"The German military recognises the potential of my research," he declared. "While your British authorities content themselves with colonial squabbles, the *patetico*, the *banale*, the mundane, the Reich prepares for the wars of the coming century—wars fought not merely with steel and powder, but with the weaponisation of the human mind itself."

Dixon smiled: "The German military evidently recognises the potential of very tight trousers, cheap perfume, and Venetian masks."

The Mechanist's face darkened, his shoulders tensing visibly as Dixon's barb struck home. For a moment, his composure faltered, replaced by a flash of raw indignation.

"You mock what you cannot comprehend, Signor Dixon," he replied, his Italian accent growing more pronounced in his agitation. "Such provincial *spirito* is precisely why your Empire teeters on the *precipizio* of obsolescence. While you trade in feeble jests, scientific progress marches forward without you."

He straightened his face, regaining his aristocratic bearing. "Let us see who laughs when the methods you deride as theatrical frivolity reshape the very fabric of civilisation. History will record your cleverness as nothing more than the dying gasp of an outmoded philosophy."

His voice lowered to a silken, menacing purr. "Besides, I find it rather amusing that a man who disguised himself as an elderly matron should dare critique my choice of attire.

Tell me, Dixon, did you select that bombazine dress for its scientific merit, or merely for the charming way it accentuated your masculine physique?"

"It was a tribute to my favourite grandmother, sir."

"Your grandmother! You are yourself the grandmother of science, Dixon! You are holding on to the diary that you cannot use like *il cane nella mangiatoia*! What's the point in all your science when you do not have the courage to use it to rule these idiots? You do not have the courage! You are a grandmother yourself, you are *una vecchia strega stupida che intralcia il vero genio, il genio dell'uomo nuovo, nella sua marcia trionfale contro i degenerati! Stupido bastardo! Ti metti in mezzo al mio genio, il genio ereditario, il vero genio dell'aristocrazia dell'Impero romano! Un barbaro! Un piccolo barbaro! Tua nonna era una puttana!*"

His diatribe was interrupted by a sudden change in his expression—his eyes widening, his words transforming into a strangled gasp as a thin wire encircled his throat, drawn taut by hands unseen behind him.

"Not so soon, *seniore*," a familiar female voice announced with deadly calm.

To my astonishment, Alice stood behind the Mechanist, her delicate hands gripping what appeared to be a guitar string that now bit deep into our adversary's flesh. Her face, normally the picture of gentle amiability, was transformed by a fierce determination I had never before witnessed.

The moment of advantage was brief. From the shadows near the window emerged the statuesque blonde whom we had observed at Alexandra Palace—the Mechanist's assistant. In her hand gleamed the metallic barrel of a lady's derringer, its diminutive size belying its lethal potential at such proximity.

"Release him," she commanded, her accent suggesting the steppes of Russia rather than the Mediterranean origins of her employer. "Or I shall be forced to ventilate your spinal column."

The few remaining patrons of the upper room, recognizing the deadly tableau unfolding before them, hastily made their departures, their footsteps clattering down the staircase in panicked retreat. As the last of them disappeared, a new figure appeared at the top of the stairs—Saeed, his normally placid countenance rendered severe by circumstance, a service revolver held with the practiced confidence of one familiar with its operation.

"I believe," he announced, training his weapon upon the Mechanist's assistant, "that we have reached what military strategists term a stalemate."

The blonde's eyes darted between Saeed and her employer, calculation evident in her expression.

"It seems," Dixon observed with remarkable sangfroid, "that our conversation has attracted a larger audience than anticipated. Perhaps, sir, you might consider lowering your weapons? I assure you, my companions will reciprocate the gesture."

For a moment, the tableau held—six individuals balanced on the knife-edge of potential violence. Then, with the careful deliberation of a chess player conceding a match, the Mechanist lowered his pistols to the tabletop.

"Very... well," he conceded, his voice hoarse from the pressure against his throat. "A temporary... accommodation... seems... *prudente*."

At a nod from Dixon, Alice released her garrote, though she maintained her position of advantage behind the Mechanist. Saeed and the blonde assistant likewise lowered their weapons, though neither returned them to concealment.

"I propose," Dixon suggested, "that we conclude our meeting and depart this establishment with a minimum of further drama. The proprietor has doubtless already dispatched a boy to summon the constabulary."

The Mechanist massaged his throat, regarding Dixon with a mixture of grudging respect and undisguised animosity. "Our business remains unfinished, Signor Dixon."

"Indeed," Dixon agreed, "though perhaps future negotiations might be conducted through less theatrical channels. I surmise you were an exotic burlesque dancer in a past life, Signor Mechanist. I can easily picture you kicking your heels at the Moulin Rouge—perhaps that's why the Swami finds you so irresistible."

The Mechanist's bile was evident in the stare that he had bestowed upon Dixon. His mask turned slightly, catching the light with a glint that made him look less like a man and more like an automaton awaiting a command.

"You misread me, Professor Dixon," he said at last, his voice velvet-wrapped steel. "But then, those who live by equations often stumble over rhythm. I forgive the confusion. Burlesque, to you, must seem chaos—when in fact it is the most intricate of choreographies. Every turn, every flourish, precisely timed. Much like a machine."

He stepped closer, lowering his voice to a whisper meant only for Dixon's ears.

"And as for the Swami... let's just say we both understand the value of a willing audience. Even your protégé, Mr. White, seems increasingly captivated by our little performances. One might almost say... seduced."

The Mechanist inclined his head slightly, then turned to the crowd with a sweeping gesture that reignited the spectacle, as though the moment of tension had never happened.

We descended the staircase in a peculiar procession, maintaining a fragile truce born of mutual vulnerability rather than trust. As we emerged into the sunlight of Highgate High Street, the Mechanist turned to Dixon with a parting observation.

"The world is changing, Signor Dixon. Those who cannot

adapt to its new realities will find themselves relegated to the fossil record of history."

Dixon's reply was measured but firm. "The most successful adaptations, sir, are those which preserve the essential characteristics of the organism while accommodating environmental pressures. Humanity's essential nature includes concepts you appear to have discarded—conscience, compassion, moral restraint."

The Mechanist's response was a smile of such genuine amusement that I found myself momentarily disarmed. "We shall see which of us reads the future more accurately, Signor Dixon."

With a courtly bow that seemed to mock the formalities it ostensibly honoured, he departed, his assistant maintaining a protective position at his flank. We watched in silence as they entered a waiting hansom cab, which immediately set off in the direction of Hampstead.

"Well," Dixon remarked, adjusting his cuffs with meticulous attention, "that was a most informative encounter."

"Informative?" I echoed, my nerves still jangling from the confrontation. "Dixon, the man threatened to shoot us both in a most delicate region!"

"A tactical error on his part," Dixon replied placidly. "Had he truly intended violence, he would have acted without preliminary discussion."

I turned to Alice, who stood beside Saeed, her composure regained, though a certain heightened colour in her cheeks betrayed her recent exertion. "Miss Trevanion, I must express my profound gratitude for your timely intervention. Though I confess myself at a loss to explain your presence here."

She exchanged a glance with Saeed before responding. "I overheard your conversation at The Gun, Mr. White. The mention of Highgate and Sunday afternoon was sufficient for me to deduce your destination. As for Mr. Saeed..." She hesitated.

"Miss Trevanion approached me with her concerns," Saeed explained. "Given our previous encounters with the Mechanist, it seemed prudent to provide additional resources for your meeting."

Dixon regarded Alice with newfound appreciation. "You have demonstrated remarkable presence of mind, Miss Trevanion. May I inquire as to where you acquired the skill of garroting?"

A shadow passed across her features. "My father was a tin miner in Cornwall, sir. Not all disputes in that industry are resolved through official channels."

I found myself viewing Alice in an entirely new light—not merely as the charming barmaid whose smile had brightened many a dismal evening, but as a woman of unexpected depths and capabilities.

Dixon, ever practical, redirected our attention to the matter at hand. "We should not linger here. The Mechanist's parting words suggested a willingness to pursue our engagement through other means."

"And what of this diary?" Saeed inquired. "Do you indeed possess such a document?"

Dixon's expression remained inscrutable. "That, my friend, is a matter for another conversation. One conducted in more secure surroundings."

As our omnibus lumbered down Highgate Hill toward the city, I found my thoughts returning to the Mechanist's unsettling discourse on the malleability of the human mind. If such manipulation were indeed possible on the scale he suggested, what terrors might the coming century hold? And what role might we, the Brothers of Koach, play in the unfolding drama of science weaponised against humanity itself?

Chapter 14
The Letter

I found my seat in the crowded lecture hall at the College, notebook in hand, doing my best to appear attentive. Goodeve's presence was almost imposing, his voice steady and resonant as he began to speak about his approach to mechanics and engineering. His concepts danced on the edge of genius and madness, hinting at universal systems of order within the chaos of motion. I scribbled notes, though they were far from coherent, the words blending together as my head began to feel heavy.

I fought to stay awake, forcing my eyes open each time they dared to close. Goodeve's voice faded in and out, the sound merging with my jumbled thoughts. Shadows of our recent encounters flickered at the edges of my mind—the stale air of the flat, Bradford's severe gaze, the sensation of iron bars clanging shut. I blinked hard, focusing on my notes, but the letters had blurred into one another.

At last, Goodeve concluded, his final words echoing through the hall. I let out a shaky breath, relieved yet still haunted by the haze of fatigue. Gathering my things, I joined the stream of students leaving the hall, each step feeling heavier than the last.

When I reached the mailroom, I approached my pigeonhole out of habit, not truly expecting anything. But there it was—a letter, half-hidden at the back, with my name neatly scrawled across the front. My pulse quickened. Could this be the response I'd been waiting for?

I tore open the envelope, my hands clumsy with anticipation, and read the brief message inside. My heart stopped as my eyes reached the signature:

"Meet me at the Bailey's Hotel at noon."

It was signed only with initials—W.K.N. There was no mistaking it. William King-Noel. The Earl of Lovelace himself.

A thrill and a flicker of dread ran through me. I glanced at my watch—it was nearly eleven. Just enough time, if I hurried. Pocketing the letter, I made my way swiftly out of the college and onto the bustling streets of South Kensington, exhaustion momentarily forgotten. Every step felt charged with significance, a magnetic pull drawing me toward Bailey's Hotel.

Chapter 15
The Meeting

The Bailey's Hotel, a grand establishment of some renown, stands proudly on Gloucester Road, its red-bricked façade an enduring testament to the ambitions of its founder, Sir James Bailey. Though its official address reads 140 Gloucester Road, its true entrance lies upon Courtfield Road, directly facing the bustling Gloucester Road underground station. A modern convenience, that underground railway—how swiftly it whisks travellers across the vast city, depositing them mere steps from Bailey's imposing doorway.

I could feel my pulse quicken as I approached the polished brass door. The instructions in the letter had been brief—too brief. And the signature, those initials, W.K.N., weighed on my mind. There was an urgency about it all that made me uneasy, but curiosity pressed me forward.

Inside, I made my way to the front desk. The receptionist, a neat woman with hair pulled tight in a bun, greeted me with a nod. "Good morning. My name is Paul White. I believe Lord King-Noel is expecting me."

The woman's expression softened, a faint trace of interest in her gaze as she scanned a ledger. "Yes, Mr. White, the Earl is waiting for you in his suite. Room 208. You may go up."

With a murmured thanks, I ascended the staircase, my heart racing in anticipation. When I reached the door to his suite, I hesitated briefly before raising my hand to knock. Almost immediately, the door swung open, and a maid, neatly dressed in black and white, appeared in the doorway.

She glanced at me with faint curiosity, then gestured for me to enter. "This way, sir. The Earl is currently resting in bed. He prefers to speak to you from behind the curtain."

A strange request, but I supposed such eccentricities were not uncommon among the aristocracy. Nobility often had their quirks, and age could only add to them. I nodded and stepped inside.

The room was dimly lit, with heavy, dark curtains drawn across the windows. A thick velvet curtain separated the bed from the rest of the suite. I could just make out the faint silhouette of a figure reclining behind it, though the curtain's fabric softened all detail. The air was tinged with an herbal scent, perhaps from some medicinal balm. I waited in the silence, feeling oddly exposed.

"Mr. White," came a voice from beyond the curtain. It was gravelly, slightly strained—appropriate for a man of King-Noel's age, yet there was something slightly off in its cadence.

"Yes, my lord," I replied, stepping a little closer. "I am Paul White. Thank you for agreeing to meet with me."

"Introduce yourself, young man. I do not know you," he said, his voice carrying a curious detachment.

Caught slightly off-guard, I offered a brief summary of my work with Dixon and my interest in Lady Ada Lovelace's diary. "I had hoped, my lord, that you might share with us any insights or artifacts you may possess related to her analytical work," I added, keeping my tone respectful.

There was a long pause. I could hear the man shift behind the curtain, a faint rustling of fabric, and then he spoke, his tone colder than before. "I am afraid you have touched upon a subject I'd rather not discuss. My marriage to Ada Lovelace was not one of joyous memories. Her work—it brought nothing but distress to our union. You will understand, Mr. White, if I ask you not to mention her again."

I faltered, taken aback. In all I'd read of King-Noel, his relationship with Lovelace was rarely discussed in such personal terms. Still, I pressed on, hesitant but determined. "My deepest apologies, my lord. I meant no offense," I said, carefully choosing my words. "I would only ask, for the sake of scientific legacy, if you might consider sharing anything you could offer on her work. I am here purely in the interest of preserving her contributions—"

"Is that how they teach manners at the Royal College of Science?" he cut in, his tone sharp with reproach. "When I was at Cambridge, fellows at the faculty I studied under knew how to respect the wishes of those older and wiser than themselves. A lesson you'd do well to learn."

The harsh rebuke stung, and I immediately felt the flush of embarrassment. "My deepest apologies, my lord," I replied, bowing my head slightly. An odd and unexpected reprimand.

Silence followed, the air thick with tension. Then, with a quiet sigh, the man spoke once more. "I think it would be best if you leave, Mr. White. I am not accustomed to guests who lack the grace to honour my wishes."

There was a pause, filled by a faint rustle from beyond the curtain. Then, suddenly, he snapped, his voice edged with impatience. "And what's that noise again? Don't tell me there is a cat at this hotel. I absolutely loathe cats."

I stood there, uncertain, a strange prickling in the back of my mind. Something about the interaction didn't sit right, yet I couldn't place what it was. I bowed again, more out of formality than respect, and murmured, "Of course, my lord. I offer my sincerest apologies once again."

Without another word, I turned and left, feeling a strange mix of disappointment and discomfort.

But the thought slipped away, buried beneath a wave of exhaustion and the sting of rebuke. I would think on it later, when my mind was clearer, when the sting of failure no longer clouded my thoughts.

Chapter 16
Revelations at The Gun

The Gun was as lively as ever, the murmur of conversation filling the cozy, smoke-filled pub as I took my usual seat near the fireplace. Alice was working her shift behind the bar, deftly filling pints and bantering with the regulars, her laugh carrying across the room. She caught my eye and, a moment later, brought over two ales, setting them down with a curious smile.

"So, what's got you in such a state, then?" she asked, sliding into the chair opposite me.

I let out a long sigh, realising I'd been holding onto my unease since that strange meeting at Bailey's Hotel. "Alice, I had a most unpleasant encounter with none other than the Earl of Lovelace."

Her eyebrows lifted. "An aristocrat, eh? Well, they're usually a disagreeable lot, aren't they?" She smirked, but I shook my head, and her smile faded.

"No, it was more than that," I replied, leaning closer, lowering my voice. "The conversation—it didn't feel right at all. Almost as though it were rehearsed."

Alice studied me thoughtfully, then reached across the table, her hand resting over mine. "It sounds to me like your intuition's trying to tell you something, Paul. Was there a word or a phrase that didn't sit right?"

I thought for a moment, the memory of that peculiar reprimand at the edge of my mind. Then, the words surfaced. "Yes... yes, there was something. The man behind the curtain mentioned the word faculty when speaking of Cambridge. He said, 'fellows at the faculty I studied under.' But that's all wrong. A true Cantabrigian would have used tripos, not faculty. It was a strange oversight."

Alice's eyes narrowed, and she nodded slowly. "And you say he's from Trinity College?"

"Yes. And what's stranger still," I continued, "was his reaction to the thought of cats. He seemed almost disgusted by them. But Trinity is known for its cats, the way they roam freely across the college grounds."

Alice leaned back, a spark of realisation in her gaze. "So whoever you met at that hotel couldn't be from Cambridge. And if he's not from Cambridge, he's certainly not the Earl of Lovelace. Someone's playing a dangerous game with you, Paul."

A chill ran through me. I took a long drink from my ale, trying to steady my nerves. "But who could want to deceive me like this? And why? The entire situation feels... unsettling." I hesitated, glancing around the room before continuing. "It's clear that someone at the College must be intercepting my letters."

Alice's expression darkened. "Someone at the College, you say? Well, there are only a handful who'd have the connections or audacity to interfere like that."

I nodded, already suspecting Goodeve's role in this strange plot. But another thought struck me—a certainty, now, that I could no longer ignore. "I must go to Ross-shire. I need to speak to the Earl himself, face-to-face, and put an end to this deception. If I can meet him on his estate, there'll be no more room for impostors or intercepted letters."

Alice watched me intently. "You're planning to go all the

way to Ben Damph Estate on your own? Are you mad?"

I glanced away, feeling a flicker of guilt. "I... I can't involve Dixon in this, Alice. He's unaware of my pursuit of the diary, and if Goodeve's after it too, I don't know who I can trust."

Alice folded her arms, her expression resolute. "Well, I'll tell you one thing, Paul White. You're not going to Ross-shire alone. You can forget about it."

I looked at her in surprise. "Alice, this is—"

"Exactly the time when you need a friend." She placed her hand on mine, squeezing it gently. "It so happens I was planning to take some time off anyway. And I'm certainly not about to let you face some imposter and his schemes alone."

I met her gaze, feeling both relieved and oddly reassured. "You'd do that, Alice? Really?"

She shrugged, a playful smile on her lips. "Well, I've been itching for a bit of an adventure. And besides," she added, her tone softening, "I'd rather not lose a good drinking partner to the schemes of some shadowy aristocrat."

I let out a laugh, the tension easing, if only for a moment. With Alice by my side, the journey to Ross-shire didn't feel quite so daunting. Together, perhaps we could uncover the truth behind this tangled web of deception.

Chapter 17
The Departure

The morning sun cast long shadows across the Huxley Building as I slipped out after my final lecture, my mind clouded by the weight of a decision I hadn't asked to make. Dixon's lessons, his guidance—all of it had shaped me more than I ever would have admitted. And yet here I was, hiding things from him in service to another man's whim. I wished Goodeve hadn't dragged me into this at all, but it was too late to turn back.

I made my way to the Penfold postbox by the building's entrance. I slipped two letters into the slot and watched them disappear with a strange sense of finality. The matter was now out of my hands, at least for the moment.

When I arrived at King's Cross, the station was a blur of movement and noise. I scanned the platform and found Alice waiting with an air of excitement barely concealed beneath her hat. Her eyes sparkled as she greeted me, though she must have sensed my mood because her expression softened.

"Ready for the journey?" she asked, her voice warm, grounding.

I nodded, though I could hardly ignore the twinge of guilt gnawing at my insides. "I am," I said, "but, Alice... I can't help feeling I've been thrown into a web of conflicting loyalties." She looked at me quizzically, and I went on, unable to keep it all inside. "Dixon is more than a mentor to me, yet here I am, hiding things from him. Goodeve put me in an impossible position, and I gave him my word. I can't break it, but it feels… wrong."

She watched me for a long moment, her expression one of understanding. "You're doing what you believe is right, Paul," she said softly. "Sometimes there's no perfect answer. But right now, you're following your own path. Maybe that's what this journey is about—finding where your loyalties truly lie."

Her words gave me some measure of comfort, but the knot in my chest only loosened as the train's whistle cut through the bustling platform. We boarded together, settling into a compartment as the train lurched forward, pulling us away from the familiar clamour of London and into the unknown.

Chapter 18
The Journey

The rhythmic clatter of the train was soothing, a metallic heartbeat that lulled the mind into strange, drifting reverie. As London faded behind us, the fields beyond the windows unfurled like a vast green scroll, dotted with cottages and slow-moving plough horses. Smoke from the locomotive curled back along the carriages, mingling with the faint scent of coal and steam oil that permeated every surface. The last trace of the city dissolved into a haze of chimneys and factory roofs, and then—quite suddenly—the countryside opened up before us, bright and endless in the morning light.

The further we travelled, the more my mind shifted from the turmoil of my promise to the thrill of the mystery ahead. For the first time in weeks, the tension that had held me seemed to ease, replaced by the faint intoxication of departure.

Alice sat beside me, her gloved hands folded neatly in her lap. She was quiet, and for a time we watched the passing world in companionable silence—the hedgerows, the scattering of sheep upon the hills, the winding rivers that gleamed like strips of beaten silver beneath the sun. Every so often the train would plunge through a cutting or a dark tunnel, and our reflections would appear in the glass—two travellers caught between worlds.

We crossed into Scotland by midday. The air seeping through the window vents grew cooler, sharper, and carried the faint tang of heather. The landscape shifted—gentler hills giving way to jagged crags and long stretches of moor, their colours sombre and noble, as though painted by an older hand. When at last we reached Edinburgh, we stepped out to stretch our legs upon the platform. The city stirred with quiet industry: porters wheeling barrows, the hiss of escaping steam, the hum of low conversation beneath the iron vaulting of the roof. Yet even amid that bustle, the place felt older, weightier—its ancient hills visible beyond the station roofs like guardians of another age.

After a short interval and a hurried luncheon of tea and bread, we resumed our journey. The second train bore us northward along the Highland line, its carriages more spartan than before. As the miles unrolled, the inhabited world seemed to fall away. Villages grew sparser; the tracks climbed through glens where the mountains pressed close, their slopes streaked with running water. Heather spread in great purple swathes across the hillsides, and the occasional red deer could be glimpsed standing motionless against the skyline.

Alice leaned forward, her face close to the window. "I've read about this land," she murmured, almost to herself. "It's strange seeing it in person. There's something... otherworldly about it."

I nodded, understanding what she meant. "It feels as though the world has grown older here," I said. "As if time itself moves differently beyond these hills."

The train rattled on through a valley washed in gold by the sinking sun. By the time we reached Inverness, dusk was falling, and a fine drizzle had begun, shrouding the distant hills in a veil of silver mist. We changed to a smaller, slower train that would carry us along the Dingwall and Skye line into Ross-shire. The difference was immediate: the carriages were narrow and draughty, the benches wooden and well-worn, the air thick with the mingled scent of damp wool and coal smoke. A solitary oil lamp swung faintly overhead, casting an amber glow upon the compartment walls.

As the train pulled away from the station, I felt the last tendrils of civilisation slip behind us. The countryside was now a wilderness—stretches of open moor broken only by the occasional loch glinting faintly in the half-light. Clusters of pine forest rose black against the horizon, their needles whispering in the wind. Once, as we passed a siding, I glimpsed a solitary crofter's hut with smoke rising from its chimney, and I wondered what life might be led in such desolate places, so far from the noise of the cities that claimed to rule the world.

The further we went, the slower the train seemed to move, as though reluctant to intrude upon the silence. At intervals we halted at small stations—Achanalt, Achnasheen—each little more than a wooden hut beside a single lamp. A few passengers alighted, disappearing into the dark with lanterns, and the rest of us continued in quiet contemplation.

Alice broke the silence at last. "It feels as though we're leaving England behind in more ways than one," she said softly.

I smiled faintly. "Perhaps that is what it means to go north," I replied. "To pass beyond the reach of reason into something wilder."

She turned to me then, her expression thoughtful. "Paul," she said, "do you truly believe we'll find the real King-Noel?"

The question startled me; it was as though she had spoken one of my own thoughts aloud. I hesitated. "I think so," I said at length. "Or at least, I think we'll find what he wanted us to find. But I'm not certain we'll like what we uncover."

Her gaze lingered on me, searching. "We'll find much more than that," she said. "But are you ready for whatever it is?"

The words hung between us, blending with the rattle of the wheels and the low whistle of the wind seeping through the joints of the carriage. I looked out at the landscape—mist rising over the heather, the pale line of a river twisting through the glen—and felt the pull of it all, strange and irresistible. My sense of loyalty warred with curiosity, duty with desire, yet the latter grew stronger with each passing mile.

"Yes," I said quietly. "We have to try. Whatever lies at the end of this journey... I need to know."

By the time we reached Achnasheen, it was near midnight. Rain fell steadily, and the station lamps shone through it like faint halos. A carriage awaited us—an old trap drawn by two sturdy Highland ponies—and our driver, a taciturn man in a worn cap, helped us aboard without a word. The horses set off at a slow, sure pace along the dark, winding road toward Torridon.

The night was utterly still save for the sound of the rain and the steady rhythm of hooves.

Mountains loomed unseen on either side, and now and then lightning flickered far off among the clouds, revealing for an instant the outlines of some vast and sleeping wilderness.

I pulled my coat tighter about me and glanced at Alice. She was gazing ahead, unflinching, her face illuminated briefly by each flash. There was no fear in her expression—only an intensity that seemed to mirror the wildness of the land itself.

We travelled on through the night, the road climbing steadily, the sea's distant murmur beginning to rise on the wind. And as we crossed the final ridge and glimpsed, far below, the faint glimmer of Loch Torridon beneath the storm, I felt a strange certainty settle over me: that our true journey—the one that would test everything we were—was only just beginning.

Chapter 19
Ben Damph Estate

As we stepped off the carriage in the village of Torridon, I felt as though we'd left behind every trace of the modern world. The landscape was both wild and serene, the mountains rising with formidable grandeur, and Loch Torridon stretched out before us, its silvery waters gleaming under a mist-veiled sky. Alice and I walked along its shores, our footsteps crunching on the gravel, our breath visible in the crisp, invigorating air.

The loch was a study in contrasts: glassy and calm near the shore, yet in the distance, its surface rippled, disturbed by the restless wind that swept through the highlands. Every so often, the sky would part, and shafts of sunlight would break through, casting a soft glow over the hills and painting the heather-strewn slopes with hints of purple and green. I was entranced, unable to resist the pull of the scenery. Each peak seemed to guard a hidden secret, each shadowed hollow a story from an ancient past. Alice walked beside me, her steps sure and steady, her gaze quietly contemplative as she took in the landscape with an inexplicable familiarity.

After nearly an hour, we finally reached the wrought-iron gates of Ben Damph Estate, the ancestral home of the Earl of Lovelace. The manor house, partly visible through a screen of old pines, was stately and imposing, with tall chimneys and gabled roofs standing out against the gray sky. As we approached, the gates creaked open, and we were met by a tall, silver-haired manservant in a dark coat. His demeanour was as brisk as the morning air, and he eyed us with a mixture of suspicion and disinterest.

"Greetings," I began, trying to project authority despite my travel-worn appearance. "I'm Paul White, from Royal College of Science, London, and this is Miss Alice—"

The manservant cut me off with a glance. "His Lordship does not accept visitors," he said curtly. His voice was polite, but there was no mistaking the finality in his tone.

I straightened, unwilling to be turned away so easily. "Please, could you inform Lord King-Noel that we've come on a matter of supreme scientific importance?" I chose my words carefully, hoping to strike a chord with the Earl's known intellectual curiosity. "It concerns his late wife, Lady Lovelace's work on analytical engines."

The manservant's expression barely shifted, though I noticed a faint narrowing of his eyes. He seemed to deliberate, then gave a brisk nod. "Wait here."

Alice and I watched him retreat along the long, winding path toward the manor. As the minutes slipped by, I grew increasingly conscious of the chill settling in. I stole a glance at Alice, who remained unbothered by the delay, looking out over the loch with calm interest.

Finally, after what felt like an eternity, the manservant returned. He regarded us with the same distant expression. "His Lordship will see you tomorrow morning at six sharp," he announced. "He likes to take his breakfast early."

With that, he turned and disappeared down the path once more, leaving the gates shut firmly behind him.

I glanced at Alice, who gave a faint smile. "Well, I suppose that means we're spending the night in Torridon," she said with a faint shrug. "Shall we head back?"

The walk back to the village was marked by a deepening sense of anticipation. With each step, I felt the weight of our journey and the purpose behind it settle heavily upon me. Though I'd tried to be diplomatic, there was a part of me that wondered if Lord King-Noel would agree to speak openly tomorrow—or if his invitation was merely a courtesy, bound to end in further obfuscation.

When we finally reached the village, dusk was settling, casting a soft glow over the small stone cottages and the smoky chimneys that rose from each. Alice led the way to a modest inn, a two-story building with a cheerful yellow door. The innkeeper welcomed us warmly, and soon enough, we found ourselves in a cozy room with a crackling fire.

Over a simple but hearty dinner, Alice and I spoke quietly, our words softened by the low murmur of other guests in the dining hall. I shared my concerns, confessing how I felt caught between my loyalties to Dixon and my promise to Goodeve. Alice listened without interruption, her gaze steady.

"Do you think he'll tell us anything?" she asked eventually, her tone thoughtful.

"I'm not sure," I admitted. "But I feel we've come too far to turn back now."

She gave a slight nod, her expression unreadable. "Well, Paul, you've managed to drag me halfway across Scotland. I suppose I'm in this with you."

I chuckled, grateful for her unwavering support. Later today, I knew, would be another test. But as I looked out through the window at the dark, quiet village beyond, I allowed myself a small glimmer of hope.

My thoughts were interrupted when the dining hall door swung open, admitting a boisterous party of locals whose voices carried the lilting cadence of the Highlands. They arranged themselves at the long table near the hearth, their conversation punctuated by hearty laughter and the occasional thump of a walking stick against the stone floor.

"Aye, MacLeod's prize bull got loose again," one of them

was saying, his weathered face creased with amusement. "Found the beast three miles down the glen, bold as brass in Mrs. Cameron's vegetable garden."

The eldest among them, a silver-haired gentleman with keen blue eyes, noticed our presence and raised his glass in our direction. "Good evening to ye, strangers. Not often we see visitors in Torridon this time of year."

I inclined my head politely. "Good evening, sir."

But it was another member of their party—a lean, sharp-featured man with suspicious eyes—who leaned forward with obvious curiosity. "And what brings ye to our remote corner of Scotland, if ye don't mind my asking?"

My mind raced. "We are Mr. and Mrs. Sutcliffe, from Bath," I replied, the lie tumbling from my lips with surprising ease. "On our wedding tour."

Alice's cheeks flushed a deep crimson, her teacup rattling slightly as she set it down. The sight of her discomfort only seemed to fuel my conviction in the deception.

The suspicious man's gaze sharpened. "Wedding tour, ye say? How... romantic."

The innkeeper, who had been listening from behind the bar, approached our table with a puzzled expression. "Begging your pardon, sir, but if ye're newly wed, why did ye request separate chambers?"

The question hung in the air like smoke from the peat fire. Alice's blush deepened, and I felt my own face growing warm. "My wife..." I began, then cleared my throat. "Mrs. Sutcliffe suffers from a most distressing condition—she talks in her sleep. Quite violently, in fact. The physicians in Bath recommended separate sleeping arrangements until a suitable treatment can be found."

Alice's eyes widened at this elaboration, but to my amazement, she rose to the occasion with remarkable aplomb. "Oh, Charles," she said, her voice trembling with what appeared to be genuine distress, "must you discuss my... my affliction before strangers?"

She pressed a handkerchief to her eyes, and I found myself momentarily stunned by the authenticity of her performance. "There, there, my dear," I murmured, placing what I hoped was a husbandly hand upon her shoulder. "The good people of Torridon need not concern themselves with such private matters."

The suspicious man's expression softened considerably. "Och, forgive me, lass. I meant no offense."

"Indeed," added the silver-haired gentleman, raising his glass once more. "To Mr. and Mrs. Sutcliffe—may your touring be pleasant and your... difficulties temporary."

The toast was echoed around the table, and gradually the conversation returned to local matters. Alice continued to play her part admirably, occasionally dabbing at her eyes and casting me looks of such convincing wifely devotion that I began to feel the deception was taking on a life of its own.

When we finally excused ourselves for the evening, Alice maintained her performance until we reached the narrow corridor that led to our respective chambers. Only when we were certain we were alone did she abandon the pretense, though the flush in her cheeks remained.

"Mrs. Sutcliffe?" she whispered, her eyes dancing with mischief. "And I talk violently in my sleep, do I?"

"It was the first excuse that came to mind," I protested, though I could not suppress a grin at her obvious amusement.

"Charles," she continued, adopting the same tone she had used downstairs, "you were quite convincing as a concerned husband." She stepped closer, her voice dropping to barely above a whisper. "The way you touched my shoulder... most husbandly indeed."

The corridor suddenly felt impossibly narrow, the space between us charged with an electricity that had nothing to do with the Mechanist's experiments. "Alice, I..."

"Good night, Mr. Sutcliffe," she said, her voice now carrying a note of gentle mockery as she reached for the handle of her door. "Do try not to worry too much about your poor afflicted wife."

She slipped into her room, leaving me standing in the dimly lit corridor, my heart racing in a manner that had nothing whatsoever to do with our recent deception. The soft click of her door closing seemed to echo in the stillness, and I remained there for several moments, trying to collect my scattered thoughts.

Finally, I made my way to my own chamber, though sleep proved elusive as I replayed every moment of Alice's performance, every glance, every carefully chosen word. The line between pretense and reality had blurred in ways I had not anticipated, leaving me to wonder what the morning might bring.

Chapter 20
The Appointment

The first light of dawn hadn't yet graced the sky when Alice and I set off along the shores of Loch Torridon. The air was crisp, and every breath seemed to carry a note of foreboding. I couldn't shake the dread pooling in my stomach, an instinctive unease I'd felt since the unsettling encounter at Bailey's Hotel.

The surface of Loch Torridon stretched out dark and glassy beside us, the moon casting its pale reflection over the water, which rippled like mercury in the slight breeze. Shadows seemed to move in the corners of my vision, only to vanish when I turned my head. Alice walked a few paces ahead, calm as ever, though I knew she sensed my tension. Her quiet confidence was comforting, but even her presence couldn't silence the doubts gnawing at me.

The Mechanist's face—or what I imagined lay behind that impenetrable mask—haunted me. My skin prickled as I remembered his deep, hypnotic voice, his assistant's inscrutable smile, and the way she'd plucked a few strands of my hair with such unsettling precision. Had it been deliberate? I wondered if, in some twisted way, I had been marked. It was a thought that only fanned the flames of my paranoia.

What if the assistant had chosen me for a reason? What if I had already crossed a line, stepping into some larger, darker scheme? The Mechanist felt less like a performer with each memory and more like a figure of menace—a shadow that had lodged itself in my mind, threatening to consume it.

My thoughts turned to Dixon. Guilt tightened my throat. What would he say if he knew I had ventured to Ross-shire without him, all because I'd given Goodeve my word? I'd always trusted Dixon to guide me, but now I was caught between him and a promise to a man I hardly knew. And in Dixon's absence, it was as though the Mechanist's shadow grew longer, creeping into every crevice of my thoughts. I could almost hear Dixon's voice, warning me against rash choices, urging caution—but here I was, drawn by some undeniable compulsion to uncover the truth, even if it meant stepping into darkness alone.

The estate loomed ahead, barely visible against the deepening shadows of the highlands. My heart pounded as we approached the gate, a hulking silhouette that seemed carved from the very mountainside. The manservant awaited us there, his figure tall and still, almost spectral in the dim predawn light. Without a word, he turned, gesturing for us to follow. I cast a quick glance at Alice, who met my gaze with a look of quiet resolve. If she sensed my anxiety, she kept it to herself, a reassuring presence by my side.

We were led through winding corridors, the walls hung with portraits that seemed to watch us as we passed. Finally, we arrived at a large, dark-panelled door. The manservant opened it without a word, standing aside to let us pass. My breath caught as I stepped into the dining room.

At the head of a long table, his back straight and his gaze sharp despite his age, sat the real William King-Noel, the Earl of Lovelace. His presence was undeniable—stoic, commanding, with an air of unyielding dignity. In the dim candlelight, his face bore the unmistakable marks of age, but his eyes held a keen intelligence that put me instantly on edge. He was, at once, everything I'd expected and yet unlike anything I could have imagined.

The manservant announced us and withdrew, leaving Alice and me standing in the vast room before the Earl of Lovelace. Silence settled over us, broken only by the faint crackle of the fire in the hearth.

"Mr. White," the Earl spoke, his voice steady, with a gravity that sent a chill down my spine. "I trust your journey was tolerable?"

It took a moment for me to find my voice. "Yes, my lord. Thank you."

He nodded, his gaze flickering between Alice and me. "I understand you've travelled here on a matter of scientific interest." His tone was calm, almost indifferent, yet I could sense an undercurrent of curiosity.

"Yes, my lord," I managed, trying to shake the unease that lingered from my thoughts. I realised, standing here, that there would be no hiding my intentions from him. The man seated before me was not one to entertain idle conversation.

"Then," he continued, folding his hands before him, "let us dispense with pleasantries, Mr. White. Tell me why you are here."

The weight of his gaze left no room for hesitation, yet for a moment, words failed me. How could I possibly convey the entangled web of secrets, loyalty, and dread that had driven me here? But, under his penetrating stare, I felt compelled to try.

Chapter 21
The Earl's Revelations

"My lord," I began, feeling strangely unsure of my words under his gaze. "I was led to believe you might have information regarding the... legacy of Lady Ada Lovelace. Specifically, her diary."

He raised an eyebrow, and I noticed a faint frown crease his brow. "I understand," he said slowly, "that Lady Lovelace's work has garnered renewed interest, though I confess I had not anticipated visitors on the matter." He paused, his gaze momentarily shifting to the far end of the room, as though burdened by some unseen memory. "This so-called 'legacy,' as you put it, has brought nothing but unrest for many who came into contact with her work."

The Earl's words were laced with something I couldn't quite place—was it grief? Weariness? I ventured forward, glancing at Alice, who gave me a slight, encouraging nod.

"I mean no intrusion, my lord," I continued carefully. "Yet, while in London, I encountered an unusual... situation. A man claiming to be you had been residing at Bailey's Hotel. He discouraged any mention of Lady Lovelace's work, and I sensed something was amiss. I believe he may have been impersonating you."

The Earl's face grew still, his gaze hardening as he processed my words. "An impersonator, you say? Intriguing, and yet... troubling." He seemed to consider this with a gravity that made me more certain of the deception. "I rarely visit London these days. My time is largely devoted to promoting the Aultbea Railway, which is of far greater importance to our Highlands than revisiting old memories in the city."

There was a measured calm in his response, but I could see the flicker of something deeper. He leaned back in his chair, hands clasped together, and regarded me intently. "So, you wish to know about Ada's work. I assume it's her diary that concerns you?"

"Yes, my lord," I replied. "Professor Goodeve at the College mentioned the diary, implying it might hold something of significance beyond what the world has yet understood. Yet, if you would rather not discuss it..."

The Earl's face softened slightly, though a shadow lingered there. "I can tell you this: Ada was a genius, undoubtedly. Her intellect was... formidable, almost to a fault. But she was an obsessed genius. And that obsession, as admirable as it was, took her down a path that ultimately left her troubled." His voice lowered, as if confessing something he'd held back for years. "Toward the end, her research grew strange, as if she'd ventured into something even she could scarcely understand. She became disturbed—unsettled."

I could hardly breathe, listening to him reveal this side of Ada Lovelace I hadn't imagined. The great mind behind the analytical engines, haunted by her discoveries? My own curiosity flared, mingling with a vague sense of dread.

"What did she discover?" I asked, my voice nearly a whisper.

The Earl hesitated, his fingers tracing the rim of his teacup. "I am not an expert in mathematics or mechanics, Mr. White, so I cannot convey the specifics. But I remember how it weighed on her." He glanced away, as though unwilling to face the memory head-on. "Ada spoke of it in fragments...

something she uncovered that defied natural order, that challenged her understanding of machines and the limits of human control. Whatever it was, it left her troubled."

A chill swept through me. Ada Lovelace, a pioneer in computation, disturbed by the implications of her own work? I felt a strange kinship to her, a fleeting understanding of that relentless drive—yet also a touch of fear.

"I believe it was around that time," the Earl continued, "that another man, a certain gentleman by the name of Michael Faraday, came to see me. He claimed an interest in Ada's research and offered a sum of money for the diary. I... did not feel it right to accept his payment." He glanced at me, his expression softening. "I trusted Faraday's reputation, and I was glad to place Ada's diary in the hands of a man of integrity. I assumed he would safeguard her work."

My mind spun at the revelation. Michael Faraday, the legendary scientist, involved with Lovelace's diary? My thoughts returned to the Mechanist and the sinister forces seemingly at work in London. This diary seemed to hold something far more profound—and far more dangerous—than mere calculations.

The Earl's gaze grew distant, as though he were retreating into a painful memory. "Ada was extraordinary, Mr. White, but not without her burdens. She bore the weight of her own mind... and, I fear, the consequences of probing too deeply into realms few others dared explore."

His voice trailed off, and I found myself deeply moved by his words. This was more than an intellectual puzzle; it was a legacy, one that seemed to come with consequences I had only begun to fathom.

The Earl straightened, the solemnity lifting slightly. "I do not wish to dwell on these matters," he said quietly. "My memories of Ada are few, but they are... kind. I remember her genius, her rare spirit, more than anything else. But I will not pretend to understand the depths of her intellect or the darkness it led her toward."

I glanced at Alice, who had been listening intently, her expression thoughtful, as if piecing together her own thoughts on what we'd heard. She caught my eye and gave a small nod, as if to say that we'd found what we came for—yet perhaps something even more.

As we rose to leave, the Earl's gaze lingered on us with an intensity I couldn't shake. "I trust you will take care, Mr. White. And if you choose to pursue this matter further..." He let the sentence hang, and a slight, sorrowful smile crossed his lips. "Well, I will leave you with that advice. Take care."

With a final nod, he gestured for the manservant, who led us silently back down the corridor. We stepped out into the cool morning air, our thoughts heavy with the Earl's revelations.

The path back to Torridon seemed longer than it had that morning. I walked beside Alice in silence, my mind replaying the Earl's words, the ghost of Ada Lovelace's legacy haunting my thoughts. Faraday, the Mechanist, Goodeve—all tangled together, all connected to her diary in ways that seemed to reach beyond our understanding. And I couldn't help but wonder... what lay ahead, and what price would be demanded for uncovering the truth?

Chapter 22
Physicists and Chemists

As we walked along the shores of Loch Torridon, my thoughts drifted to Michael Faraday, whose brilliance lay in his relentless curiosity, his insatiable need to probe the nature of forces unseen. He had single-handedly propelled the study of electromagnetism into the realm of practical science. It was his work that laid the foundation for the engines, dynamos, and transformers that now pulsed in factories across the world. What's more, Faraday had done it all without formal education or social privilege—proof, if ever there was, that genius was a force unto itself, unconcerned with status or lineage.

But Faraday's discoveries had also drawn rivals. As I walked, names flickered across my memory—figures of equal renown and fierce ambition.

There was Nikola Tesla, the enigmatic Serbian with his towering inventions and visionary mind. Tesla's work on alternating current had revolutionised electrical transmission, yet he was a man known for his eccentricities as much as his genius. I wondered what Tesla would have thought of Faraday's diary, or if he had ever been privy to it. Tesla, with his grand dreams and uncanny ability to envision machines no one else could comprehend, seemed somehow the perfect heir to Faraday's legacy—yet he had followed a different path, one that often clashed with the sensibilities of the scientific establishment.

And then there was Alexander Popov, the Russian physicist known for his work on radio waves. Popov had pursued wireless communication with a passion that bordered on obsession. Unlike Tesla, he had approached his work with a strict, systematic method that mirrored Faraday's own approach. I could see why Popov might have admired Faraday, even if they'd never met; both men had that rare quality of seeing into the unknown, of taking the intangible and making it real.

Of course, no list of Faraday's rivals would be complete without Thomas Edison. Edison, ever the shrewd businessman, had turned his scientific prowess into wealth and influence unmatched by his peers. For Edison, science was a tool, a means to an end, and he pursued his discoveries with an energy that bordered on ruthlessness. Where Faraday's work had been motivated by a pure, almost ascetic love of discovery, Edison's was often directed by financial gain. I couldn't imagine Edison having any interest in Lovelace's diary unless he believed it held some immediate, profitable secret.

And finally, there were the Marconi brothers: first, the young prodigy Guglielmo, then Alfonso, Luigi, and finally Dominico. The name Marconi now evoked images of wireless signals travelling across the vast Atlantic, messages leaping through the air as if by magic. But Dominico—the mysterious, elusive fourth Marconi brother—had always been a shadowy figure. His name had all but vanished from history, a footnote in the lives of his famous siblings after his untimely death in a boating accident. His body was never recovered.

Lost in thought, I realised Alice was looking at me, her eyes curious. "What's on your mind, Paul?" she asked gently.

"Faraday," I replied, my voice a little breathless, the weight of his legacy filling me with both admiration and apprehension. "It's remarkable to think that he may have held

Lovelace's diary, that a man of his integrity could have been the one to protect it. And yet..." I hesitated, a sense of dread creeping into my thoughts. "And yet, something about this feels... wrong."

Alice nodded, understanding. "Do you think Faraday could have used the diary's knowledge?"

"It's hard to say," I admitted. "Faraday was beyond reproach, a man of science in the purest sense. But those who came after him... well, they might not have shared his motives. Tesla, Edison, the Marconis—they were part of a new wave, one that saw the power in Faraday's discoveries but also the profit. And in the case of Dominico Marconi..." I trailed off, remembering the odd, forgotten details of Dominico's life. "Who knows what he might have become if he hadn't vanished? His brothers went on to change the world, but he..."

I stopped, unable to find the words. Alice was quiet, her expression thoughtful. We walked on in silence, the weight of history pressing in around us, and I couldn't shake the feeling that, somehow, we were treading a path that had been walked before—a path that led into shadows I wasn't sure we were prepared to face.

Chapter 23
The Trap Unveiled

We spent another night in the village of Torridon. The light was just beginning to spill across the Scottish hills when Alice and I settled down to breakfast at the small inn. The morning felt unusually calm, the quiet murmur of voices and clink of dishes adding a warmth to the chilly air. I was deep in thought, my mind lingering over our meeting with the Earl, piecing together fragments of Ada's life, the diary, and the strange, veiled mention of Michael Faraday.

Alice glanced up from her cup, a look of dawning alarm overtaking her usual calm. "Paul," she said, lowering her voice. "You'd better see this."

She held out a copy of the morning paper, its thin pages rustling as she turned it toward me. I took it, feeling a slight unease as my gaze fell on a headline that nearly sent the blood rushing from my head:

"Head of Murdered Magician Found in Professor Dixon's Office"

My stomach dropped. As I scanned the article, a chill swept over me.

It recounted the gruesome details with a clinical coldness, noting how the beheaded body of Bartolomeo Bertini—an infamous magician with a shadowy reputation—had been discovered a few days earlier in the flat above Pinoli's Restaurant. But this wasn't the shock that held me frozen in my seat. It was the revelation that, following an anonymous tip-off, the severed head had been found in none other than Professor Dixon's office at the Royal College of Science. "Dixon," the article went on, "who is rumoured to have ties with London's darker underbelly, is now in custody at Newgate Prison, where he awaits questioning."

Alice was studying my face, her eyes full of worry. "Paul," she said gently, "is there any chance Dixon could have been involved?"

I shook my head, trying to quell the rising panic in my chest. "It doesn't make sense. Dixon may have his... unusual interests, but he's not a killer."

But even as I said it, uncertainty gnawed at me. Dixon's fascination with the Mechanist had been all-consuming, his theories growing darker and more obsessive with each passing week. Had I been blind to a side of him that I hadn't wanted to see? My mind raced, piecing together fragments of the Mechanist's sinister performance and the severed head's eerie semblance to Bertini.

"What if..." I murmured, almost to myself, "this is a trap?"

Alice raised an eyebrow. "What do you mean?"

I clenched the newspaper, my knuckles whitening. "The Mechanist—Bertini—whatever he was. He must have set this up, planted his own head to incriminate Dixon and eliminate a rival. It's almost... brilliant, in a twisted way."

Alice looked skeptical but thoughtful. "So, you think the Mechanist wanted to frame Dixon? Why would he go to such lengths?"

"Because Dixon was on his trail," I replied, a bitterness creeping into my voice. "They were like two chess players, each manoeuvring to outwit the other. And now... now Dixon's in Newgate Prison, likely paying the price for underestimating his opponent."

I felt Alice's hand cover mine, her warmth grounding me

amidst the swirl of doubts and fears. "Then we need to get back to London," she said firmly. "If this Mechanist is powerful enough to set up Dixon, he won't stop there."

I nodded, pushing aside my breakfast. "We'll take the first train. I can't let Dixon face this alone, not when he's been so wrongly accused."

But even as I said the words, a sliver of doubt remained, haunting me like a shadow. Could Dixon truly be innocent, or was there something he hadn't told me—something far darker than I was prepared to believe?

Without another word, Alice and I gathered our things, and as the first rays of dawn brightened the Scottish landscape, we hurried to the station, driven by a shared urgency and a newfound fear that London held far darker secrets than I had ever imagined.

Chapter 24
Michael Faraday

As the train rocked gently along the tracks, I found myself staring out at the shifting scenery, colours blurring together in the early dawn light. I tried to settle into my seat and close my eyes, willing myself to rest. But sleep wouldn't come. My thoughts kept racing, circling back to the same doubts and questions. How could I hope to survive the world of science, filled as it was with rivalry and intrigue? What chance did I have against minds like Faraday's, giants who had reshaped entire fields of knowledge?

Michael Faraday… now there was a man to admire. He hadn't been born into wealth or privilege, nor had he walked the well-trodden paths of university halls like so many of his peers. Faraday's education had begun humbly, in a London bookbinder's shop, where he spent his days surrounded by the smell of leather and the rough feel of paper. It was there that he discovered science, not from formal instruction but from books he devoured between binding orders. Reading through these volumes, he grasped at secrets buried in pages others considered mere trade tools.

I thought of the challenges he'd faced—how, despite his lack of formal training, he'd caught the attention of Sir Humphry Davy at the Royal Institution. Faraday's perseverance and insatiable curiosity led him to become Davy's assistant, a position that opened doors to scientific exploration he might otherwise never have dreamed possible. But it was more than opportunity that set him apart. Faraday had a kind of vision, a way of looking at the natural world that cut straight to the heart of mystery.

In his lifetime, Faraday's discoveries reshaped modern science. I could almost recite them from memory, having read and re-read his works, hoping to glean some measure of his genius. He had unlocked the principles of electromagnetic induction and invented the first electric motor, showing that electricity and magnetism were intertwined in ways no one had imagined before. Faraday's laws of electrolysis explained how chemical compounds dissolved in an electric field, a revelation that turned the tables on chemistry itself. And, of course, there was his groundbreaking work on magnetic fields and dielectric materials, which led to his invention of the Faraday cage—a cage that could shield whatever it held from external electric fields, a concept that still bore his name.

One of his last accomplishments, nearly an afterthought, had been a passing involvement with one of the earliest sound-recording devices. It hadn't been his design, but Faraday was quick to appreciate its potential: a machine capable of capturing the human voice, of storing and preserving sounds beyond a fleeting moment. I wondered how he would have felt seeing an early phonograph here on this very train, carrying voices across decades like phantoms of the past.

I shifted in my seat, running through each of his triumphs, hoping to quell the persistent knot of self-doubt in my chest. Diamagnetism, the Faraday effect, benzene, polarisation—the list of his discoveries seemed endless. And all of this from a man with no formal scientific training. A self-taught prodigy who went on to change the very fabric of scientific understanding.

I closed my eyes, seeing Faraday's achievements as if they were playing out before me in fragments, each discovery a flicker of insight, a burst of light from the darkness of ignorance. And yet, beneath the awe I felt for him, there was a gnawing question: Could I ever make a mark in science? Did I have the resolve to withstand the inevitable rivalries, the jealousies and misunderstandings?

The sharp blast of the train whistle jolted me back to the present, breaking through my thoughts. I blinked, seeing the landscape through the window again, now painted in the soft hues of early morning. Alice shifted beside me, glancing over as if she could sense my unrest. I forced a small smile, nodding at her before I turned my gaze back out to the fields rushing past, holding onto the image of Faraday and all that he'd achieved—hoping, somehow, to borrow a bit of his courage.

Chapter 25
Back at Newgate Prison

As I entered the austere halls of Newgate Prison, a chill ran through me. The towering stone walls, the dank smell, the oppressive silence broken only by the occasional clanging of a gate—it felt like stepping into a tomb. Today, however, I was here not as an inmate but as a visitor, though the line felt thin as I approached the heavy iron door that led to the cells.

At Sir Edward Bradford's insistence, I was granted this brief meeting with Dixon. But it was clear that Bradford's influence had its limits; there was an air of tension, as if the guards themselves weren't certain if Dixon would remain a visitor much longer. As I was led to his cell, I caught a glimpse of him through the metal bars, his form unmistakable, stoic as ever, though a bit thinner, paler, and quieter than I'd ever seen him.

We faced each other through the railings. Dixon looked at me with a faint smile, one that didn't quite reach his eyes.

"Ah, Paul," he greeted, his voice low, steady, but tinged with something heavier, "even Bradford won't be able to undo this one. The noose is practically tied, unless you can find the real murderer—the Mechanist." He tried to chuckle, but the sound came out hollow, shadowed by an undeniable dread.

"Professor, you don't deserve this. There has to be some

way..." I started, my voice trembling despite myself.

Dixon shook his head, a slight smirk playing at his lips. "In science, Paul, we understand reality without illusions. Despite my experience, I find I'm not quite ready to meet it at the gallows." His voice softened, and he leaned forward, slipping something small through the bars. "Here. Keep this safe."

I stared down at the object he passed to me, hardly daring to breathe as I recognised the faded leather cover, the delicate scrawl pressed into its spine. Lovelace's diary. The original.

"Professor..." I stammered, caught between awe and confusion. "How did you even manage to bring this into Newgate?"

Dixon cut me off with a quick, sharp glance, his eyes darting to the guard in the distance. "No questions, Paul. This book... it's dangerous. More than you know. Don't follow Faraday's mistake. If it comes to a choice between your life and the diary, choose to live."

I opened the booklet carefully, just enough to glimpse the pages inside. Diagrams spiraled across the paper, dense and intricate; mathematical formulae laced between notes, sketches, and what appeared to be encrypted lines of text. It was like gazing into Ada's mind, her secrets captured in ink—a scientific masterpiece, perhaps, but laced with a mystery I barely understood.

"Professor..." I whispered, the weight of the booklet in my hand feeling heavier than its physical form.

Before Dixon could reply, the sudden sound of footsteps shattered the quiet. A guard approached, his expression a mixture of disdain and indifference. "Time's up."

Dixon gave me a final, fleeting look, his gaze clear and resolute even as the guard took him by the arm. "Remember, Paul," he called over his shoulder as they led him away, "the diary can reveal many things—but it will demand a price. Be careful what you seek."

I slipped the diary into my coat pocket, my heart pounding as I felt its edges press against me. My mind was racing with questions, with fear, with the enormity of what Dixon had entrusted to me. As the guard led me away from the cell block, I knew that whatever path lay ahead, it had already shifted—drawn deeper into a mystery.

Chapter 26
Waiting on the Elm Tree

The lecture hall was stifling, though I knew it was only my own mind that had turned it into a prison. I barely registered the lecturer's voice or the steady scratch of pens on paper around me. Outside these walls, Dixon was sitting in a cell, awaiting the inevitable. I'd tried my best to concentrate, to will myself into the present, but my thoughts strayed constantly to Newgate, to the cryptic words he'd left me with, and to the diary—Ada's diary—hidden beneath my coat, weighing heavier on me than I'd expected.

The lecture ended with a scrape of chairs, but I stayed frozen for a moment, watching students file out. I made my way through the building, stopping just outside Professor Neil Fowler's office. I knocked quietly, glancing over my shoulder, though I wasn't sure why. Something in the air around the Huxley Building felt charged, and I couldn't shake the sense that eyes were following my every step. Finally, the door opened, and Professor Fowler, with a knowing look, ushered me inside.

His office was a world of quiet and order. Books lined the walls in tidy rows, an island of calm in the storm raging within my mind.

"Ah, Paul," Professor Fowler said, his tone casual. "I've heard of your mentor. What a terrible story."

I looked at the floor.

"I assume you know why I'm here, Professor?" I managed.

He nodded, reached under his desk, and brought out a small black suitcase. It was nondescript, unmarked, almost too ordinary. He placed it on the desk between us.

"Please return it as soon as you've finished with it," he said, his voice low, steady, and devoid of any further explanation.

"Of course," I replied. I took the suitcase, nodded in acknowledgement, and left his office.

The weight of the suitcase felt almost oppressive in my hand as I left the Huxley Building, its simple shape somehow foreign, even foreboding. I'd been told by Dixon to trust Fowler, yet carrying it felt as though I were cradling something delicate, even dangerous.

I crossed the grounds quickly, slipping through the throng of students and making my way toward Hyde Park. The city unfolded around me in its usual noisy, bustling self, blissfully unaware of the strange machinery of secrets it hid beneath its skin.

I entered the park and cast a quick glance around, noting the familiar layout of the open paths, the groves of trees, and the lake in the distance. The air was warm, filled with the sounds of children playing and the chatter of passersby. I tightened my grip on the suitcase and made my way to a tall elm tree that stood overlooking the Orangery. It was slightly off the main path, surrounded by bushes and overgrown ivy—a place I could observe from without being seen.

Satisfied that no one was watching, I slipped off my coat, slung the suitcase carefully over my shoulder, and began to climb. It wasn't a difficult ascent, but the added weight made each branch feel precarious, each movement calculated. Finally, I settled on a sturdy branch, the suitcase beside me, my back pressed against the trunk. The leaves above shaded me from the midday sun, casting dappled shadows over the suitcase and me. I looked out over the park, feeling a strange sense of anticipation.

All I had to do now was wait.

From my vantage point, I could see the entrance to the Orangery, the steady stream of people moving in and out, their figures reduced to faint blurs by the distance. My mind wandered, racing through the events of the past few days. The weight of the diary at my hip, hidden beneath my coat, reminded me of the responsibility I carried. The notebook Dixon had entrusted to me was full of secrets—Ada's secrets, Dixon's secrets, secrets that could change everything. And the thought terrified me.

I closed my eyes briefly, trying to clear my mind. But memories and fears flooded in—the image of Dixon's weary smile as he handed me the diary, his cryptic warnings, the chilling possibility of his guilt. Could I trust him fully, knowing how deep his obsession with the Mechanist ran? Could I even trust myself in this labyrinth of deception and scientific rivalry?

A shiver ran through me, breaking the stillness. I opened my eyes, watching the horizon where the trees met the sky. The minutes stretched, and my thoughts turned to Faraday, to Ada's work, to the long line of men and women who had dared to push the boundaries of science and the price they had paid for it. Was I willing to pay that price? Could I survive in a world where brilliance and betrayal seemed to walk hand in hand?

A faint sound snapped me from my thoughts—a train whistle in the distance, low and haunting, as if carried on some invisible wind.

Chapter 27
The No-Show

Just before I left for Scotland, I had sent two letters. One was sent to Professor Neil Fowler. The other was addressed to Dixon, though I'd made a deliberate error in the address, substituting his full name with his initials. A hasty mistake, it would seem. But I knew all too well that my letters were being intercepted, that someone was reading them before they ever reached their intended hands. This time, I wasn't trying to communicate with Dixon. I was laying a trail, a faint breadcrumb for the true audience—the one lurking in the shadows.

I had written something cryptic yet unmistakable, hinting that I would be waiting at the Orangery, holding an object of significant interest. The object of which *he* was aware. If the wrong eyes found the letter, I knew they would understand exactly what I meant.

Perched up in the elm tree, I kept my gaze fixed on the entrance to the Orangery, the steady throng of people blurring together, no one appearing particularly unusual or familiar. The minutes dragged, and I could feel the anticipation humming through me, my pulse quickening with each passing second. The thought that I might be able to lure out my pursuer, to finally catch them red-handed, was tantalizing.

Then, a familiar flash of ginger hair caught my eye—just a glimpse, but unmistakable. I knew that figure instantly: it was Goodeve's assistant. He was scanning the area, his gaze flicking from side to side, eyes sharp and wary, as if expecting something.

I stayed still, barely daring to breathe. I waited, watching as he circled the area once, then twice. Finally, as he paused, apparently satisfied that his "meeting" would not happen, I made my move. Slowly, with calculated silence, I descended the tree, one foot after the other, keeping an eye on him as he turned to leave. My heart pounded as I slipped to the ground, keeping low behind the underbrush. When I was certain I was out of sight, I straightened up, walking briskly toward the park's edge.

Once I'd put sufficient distance between us, I let out a shaky breath. I hadn't expected Goodeve's assistant, of all people, but it made sense. He'd been shadowing me at the professor's behest, nudging me toward answers without ever explicitly revealing his own hand—and his ginger head. And now, he'd been drawn out by the bait.

I checked my watch and realised, with a jolt, that I was running late. I picked up my pace, making my way quickly back to the Docklands. Alice would be waiting for me at The Gun, and I had promised to meet her there. She'd worry, and rightly so, if I didn't show up on time.

As I made my way through the streets, the day's events churned through my mind, puzzle pieces rearranging themselves, new images forming with each step. One thing was clear: I was being closely watched. And if I was going to navigate this web of intrigue and misdirection, I needed to stay one step ahead. But tonight, I'd find a brief reprieve in Alice's company. For now, that would be enough.

Chapter 28
Meeting with Alice

The Gun was bustling with its usual crowd, the clinking of glasses and the low hum of conversation filling the warm, wooden interior. I found Alice near the fireplace, a hint of a smile lighting up her face when she spotted me. She leaned forward as I sat down, a glint of intrigue in her eyes.

"I did a bit of asking around," she began, keeping her voice low enough to blend with the murmur of the pub. "And it turns out our Italian triplets were indeed seen in the Docklands. Specifically, at the Bow Creek Arms."

I raised an eyebrow, impressed by her resourcefulness. "And who exactly gave you that information?" I asked, only half-joking.

Alice laughed, a quiet, mischievous sound. "Oh, they weren't exactly hard to spot," she replied. "Apparently, three Italian men who look exactly alike tend to draw attention around here."

I let her words settle, already weighing the implications. The Bow Creek Arms was near Trinity Buoy Wharf—a little too close, considering Dixon's entanglement and the Mechanist's performances. But before I could mull it over further, Alice reached across the table, her hand clasping mine tightly.

"Promise me, Paul," she said, her voice dropping even lower, tinged with concern. "Don't go to Trinity Buoy Wharf alone. Call the police. Please."

I shook my head, forcing myself to keep my tone steady. "Alice, we both know that won't work. I'm Dixon's associate, probably a suspect by now. The police would hardly take my word for it, even if I went with solid evidence. Besides..." I hesitated, glancing around the room to ensure no one could hear, "I have reason to believe the Mechanist has some of them in his pocket."

Her grip on my hand tightened, her knuckles turning pale. She looked away for a moment, clearly weighing her words, before turning back to me with a softness in her gaze I hadn't expected.

"Then," she murmured, "for luck."

And, just like that, she leaned in and gave me a quick kiss on the cheek, her lips brushing my skin in a way that sent a subtle, grounding warmth through me.

I smiled, feeling her warmth bolster my resolve. "Thank you, Alice. That may just be what I need."

The weight of what lay ahead pressed down on me as I finished my drink, but Alice's gesture—simple, sincere—somehow made it feel just a little lighter.

Chapter 29
Trinity Buoy Wharf

Trinity Buoy Wharf was alive with movement, the sounds of crates shifting, ropes tightening, and the occasional blast of a foghorn filling the air. The steady pulse of industry was inescapable, as was the smell—briny, metallic, and tinged with smoke. I clutched the small black suitcase, feeling its weight not just in my hand but in the significance it held. Lovelace's diary was now inside, hidden among Professor Fowler's gadgets, which I had yet to examine.

As I made my way past bustling workers and the towering forms of cranes, I could almost feel the history embedded in the very stones beneath my feet. This place was more than just a shipping hub; it was a site of innovation, a crossroads where science met the sea. It was here, in a nearby warehouse, that Faraday himself had once worked under the commission of the Trinity House. His task had been practical—finding better ways to illuminate England's coastlines and save mariners from disaster. And yet, in his unassuming manner, he had opened new frontiers in electromagnetism and optics.

Faraday had experimented with light in ways that seemed almost mystical—testing different gases, manipulating lenses, discovering the subtle dance of particles as they emitted and absorbed light. His work here was practical, yes, but visionary as well. That a man so humble, so dedicated to understanding the natural world, had walked these very docks was something I found both grounding and daunting.

As I turned down one of the wharf's narrower paths, something caught my eye. Three identical figures were moving through the crowd, their dark coats and wide-brimmed hats making them stand out among the dock workers. The Italian triplets. Instinctively, I pressed myself behind a large buoy, half-obscured by crates stacked beside it, and watched as they ambled down toward the Bow Creek Arms. They paused briefly, exchanging words in low, hurried voices before disappearing through the pub's narrow doorway.

I took a deep breath, waiting for a moment to make sure they were well inside. This was my chance. Stepping back out onto the path, I made my way toward the lighthouse, the suitcase feeling heavier with each step.

The lighthouse loomed ahead, its form both imposing and strangely welcoming. It was isolated from the more chaotic parts of the wharf, its iron railings and solid brick structure standing like a sentinel at the edge of the world. I quickened my pace, feeling a strange sense of anticipation mingled with dread. Whatever answers lay within these walls, they would bring me closer to understanding the Mechanist—and perhaps, closer to the truth behind Dixon's predicament and Lovelace's enigmatic work.

Chapter 30
At the Lighthouse

As I slipped into the lighthouse, I found the door surprisingly unlocked. The ground floor was cluttered with electronic devices and chemical equipment, an odd assortment that felt both dated and advanced. The air was thick with the faint, acrid smell of chemicals and old circuitry, and I realised with a thrill that I was likely standing in the remnants of Faraday's laboratory. This was where he had worked, where he had conjured the ideas that laid the groundwork for modern science.

A winding staircase rose in the corner, leading to the floor above. I climbed, gripping the railing, my heartbeat quickening with every step. As soon as my head emerged at the top of the staircase, a voice cut through the air, smooth and chilling.

"Mr. White! We have been expecting you."

Standing in the shadows, the Mechanist was a tall, imposing figure. He sat behind a large desk, strewn with strange contraptions and open books. With a composed grace, he rose and walked towards me. I steadied myself, took a deep breath, and said, "Good evening, Signor Dominico Marconi."

The reaction was immediate; his face paled, his confident demeanour faltering for just a second. I pressed on, my voice unwavering. "The missing fourth Marconi brother. You are a spitting image of your more famous and successful brother, Signor."

But Dominico recovered quickly, an icy smile creeping

onto his face. "Fool!" he spat. "Now you have brought me that, which I have been looking for all along among Faraday's belongings. Give me Lovelace's grimoire!"

Keeping my gaze steady, I knelt down and placed the black suitcase on the floor, opening it to reveal Lovelace's diary. I lifted it slowly, making sure his attention was riveted on it. "Only if you prove Dixon's innocence in the murder of your teacher, Bartolomeo Bertini," I demanded, my voice as steady as I could muster. "The teacher whom you have murdered in order to take his place."

Dominico's expression turned hard, his voice dripping with contempt. "Impossible. Dixon is a threat. The gallows are the best place for him. Bertini was only a tool to vanquish Dixon. And now I will vanquish you, danno collaterale."

The finality in his tone ignited a fury within me, and before I knew it, we were locked in a physical struggle. Dominico was strong—surprisingly strong—but Dixon's boxing lessons came back to me, guiding my movements. With a surge of adrenaline, I shoved him towards the winding staircase. Dominico staggered, then lunged back, grabbing a fistful of my shirt, dragging me down with him. We tumbled down the spiral staircase, hitting the ground floor with a bone-jarring crash, Dominico pinned beneath me.

I lay there, gasping for breath, my body aching from the fall. Dominico, slightly bloodied and winded, turned his head towards me, a malicious gleam in his eyes. He whispered, "If I die, Dixon will certainly hang."

As I struggled to pull myself up, I caught a glimpse of slender legs stepping into view. A pair of scarlet heels. I looked up to find Marconi's assistant standing over us, her outfit a startling contrast to the gloom of the lighthouse.

Before I could react, she produced a strand of hair from her corset, her movements quick and precise. She held it up to the light, a cruel smile tugging at her lips. Then, with a flick of her fingers, she lit the hair on fire.

A searing pain exploded at the top of my head, the flame catching my hair as I writhed in agony, trying to smother it with my hands. The burning sensation was unbearable, and it took every ounce of strength not to scream as I struggled to put out the flames. My vision blurred from the pain, and it was only after a moment that I realised the agony had subsided. I lay on the ground, breathing heavily, disoriented, and utterly drained.

When I regained my senses, they were gone—Marconi and his assistant had vanished, leaving only the faint echo of their steps fading into the distance. Thankfully, the black suitcase was where I had left it at the top of the staircase. But Lovelace's diary was nowhere to be found. It was now in the hands of Marconi and his accomplices.

Chapter 31
Sir Edward Bradford

I stood in Sir Edward Bradford's office, each breath coming heavy and uneven, each one a painful reminder of my encounter at the lighthouse. Bradford sat behind his imposing oak desk, observing me with that unwavering, assessing gaze of his, while shadows from the gas lamps flickered across the room, giving everything a strange, wavering quality.

"Mr. White," Bradford began, his voice carrying the gravity of someone who knew too well how the wheels of justice ground down on people. "I commend your loyalty to Professor Dixon. But you must understand—the press and the public are demanding a culprit. They want someone to pay for the crime, and Professor Dixon, with his... peculiar reputation, is their perfect target. As much as I value his contributions in our previous cases, I can't help him without undeniable proof."

I swallowed, the metallic taste of nerves still lingering on my tongue. My hand shook slightly as I unclasped the small black suitcase I'd brought, every movement heavy with the weight of all that had led to this moment. I knew Bradford wouldn't believe it at first, but I was counting on the device to do what words alone never could.

I carefully lifted the miniature phonograph from the suitcase and placed it on his desk. Its polished metal gleamed softly in the lamplight, a device as inconspicuous as it was extraordinary. Bradford's brow furrowed as he regarded it, his expression equal parts intrigue and skepticism.

"A phonograph," I explained, trying to keep my voice steady. "A miniature one. It recorded my entire conversation with Dominico Marconi—the Mechanist."

Bradford blinked, momentarily thrown off-balance. "Recorded... the conversation? You're telling me this device captures voices?"

I nodded, meeting his skeptical gaze with a look I hoped conveyed the gravity of what I was about to reveal. "Every word, Sir Edward. The entire exchange, including Marconi's admission that he framed Dixon. This"—I tapped the phonograph—"is our proof."

He leaned forward, studying the device as if it were some kind of enchanted object. "Remarkable," he muttered, reaching out with an almost reverent caution. "If this works, it could transform the way we administer justice. A device that records voices... the implications are... staggering."

"Let me show you," I said, and wound the mechanism, pressing the small switch to play. The phonograph whirred to life, and then—quiet but clear—my own voice filled the room, followed by Marconi's low, chilling tones. Every word was preserved, the entire conversation crackling faintly yet undeniably through the machine. My accusations, his twisted confessions—it was all there, as real and damning as the events themselves.

As the recording played, I watched Bradford's face. At first, he was impassive, leaning forward, listening intently. But as Marconi's words poured out, his expression shifted. By the end, he looked almost astonished, as if he had just glimpsed the future.

When the device fell silent, I exhaled, the tension finally easing out of me. Bradford sat back, shaking his head slowly. "This is... this is astonishing, Mr. White." His voice held a note of awe. "You've given us proof that even the most cunning criminals can't escape. Technology like this... it could reshape justice itself."

He rose, his gaze softening as he placed a firm hand on my shoulder. "With this evidence, Dixon's name will be cleared. You've done more than save him, Paul. You may have just changed the entire landscape of how we seek truth."

Chapter 32
The Explosion

I drifted off to sleep quickly that night, my mind alight with the events of the past day. The struggle with the Mechanist had left my muscles sore, my scalp aching enormously, and my mind buzzing, yet the meeting with Bradford lingered in my thoughts even more. I lay there in the quiet of the basement room at Nelson House, replaying our conversation until sleep finally claimed me.

I don't know how long I'd been asleep when I felt it. At first, it seemed like a vibration on the very edge of consciousness, like a distant memory. But the tremors grew, shaking the bed beneath me, strong enough to rattle the glass on the small window overhead. I blinked, struggling to piece together what was happening. The floor itself seemed to heave, as though the earth were alive and restless beneath the foundations.

And then a loud bang—a single, sharp crack of sound from above, followed by the unmistakable crash of breaking glass. I sat bolt upright, my pulse pounding as fragments of plaster dust sifted down from the ceiling. Books toppled from the shelves around me, thudding onto the floor as if thrown by an unseen hand.

"An earthquake," I murmured, the words feeling absurd on my tongue. Earthquakes in London were rare, almost unheard of. But the evidence lay around me, undeniable in its violence.

I braced myself as the walls groaned, a final, fading shudder passing through the room before stillness returned. For a moment, I simply sat there, waiting, half-expecting the tremors to begin again. But silence settled over the house, punctuated only by the faint sound of broken glass tinkling somewhere above.

I rose, my hands still trembling, and surveyed the scattered books at my feet. Whatever had just happened, it was unlike anything I'd ever felt before.

A sudden, terrible thought struck me. What if this wasn't an earthquake at all? My mind raced to the Mechanist, to Trinity Buoy Wharf. I threw on my clothes with fumbling haste, my heart hammering against my ribs. Something was terribly wrong.

The night air hit me like a splash of cold water as I burst onto the street. I ran along Cold Harbour, nearly colliding with a bleary-eyed occupant of the nearby house who had also been shaken from sleep. "Did you feel that?" he demanded, his voice thick with confusion and alarm.

"Yes," I called over my shoulder. "I need to see what's happened."

The sky to the east glowed with an unnatural light—not the soft illumination of dawn, but a fierce, flickering orange that painted the clouds with an ominous hue. Others had emerged from their homes as well, faces upturned in wonder and alarm at the strange luminescence.

"Fire!" someone shouted from further down the street. "There's a fire at the docks!"

My fears crystallised into certainty. I began to run, my footsteps echoing in the darkened streets as I made my way toward the river. The glow in the sky grew brighter with each step, and soon I could smell it—the acrid tang of burning wood and something else, something chemical and sharp that burned my nostrils and sent a chill through me despite my exertion.

As I rounded the corner onto the main road leading to

the docks, I saw it. Across the dark expanse of the Thames, Trinity Buoy Wharf was ablaze. Flames reached into the night sky like grasping fingers, consuming the structures that had stood for decades, illuminating the water with their terrible reflection. The lighthouse—the very same building where I had confronted the Mechanist—was engulfed, its once-sturdy form transformed into a pillar of fire.

I stood transfixed, my chest heaving from the run, watching as sparks spiraled upward into the smoke-choked air. All around me, people gathered, their faces ghoulishly lit by the distant conflagration.

"What happened?" a woman beside me asked, her voice thin with shock.

"An explosion," someone else replied. "Heard it clear as day. Felt it too—like the ground itself was shaking."

An explosion. My mind raced back to the Mechanist, to Dominico Marconi. Was he involved in this somehow?

"The chainhouse," a gruff voice said from nearby. "That's where it started. Something in there went up like a powder keg."

A fire barge was already making its way across the water, its lights cutting through the smoke, but it was clear that the effort was futile.

I watched, mesmerised by the terrible beauty of it, as the flames continued their relentless consumption. The heat from the fire was palpable even from this distance, warming my face as I stood among the growing crowd of onlookers. Fire engines arrived, their bells clanging through the night, but their efforts seemed pitiful against the maelstrom across the water. This was no ordinary fire; this was destruction on a scale that seemed almost biblical, as though some divine judgement had been passed upon the wharf.

As I watched, a section of the lighthouse's upper structure collapsed in a shower of sparks and burning debris. A collective gasp rose from the crowd. The symbol of safety and guidance for countless mariners was being consumed before our eyes, its light not a beacon but a pyre.

As dawn broke, casting its pale light over the still-burning ruins, I turned away. I returned to Nelson House for some much needed rest.

Chapter 33
Dinner at Rules

The dining room at Rules presented itself to me as an exhibition of English opulence—a vision of crimson and mahogany that seemed to embrace us upon our entrance. The chandeliers cast a most agreeable luminance throughout the chamber, their crystal pendants refracting the gaslight into countless points of brilliance that danced upon the polished surfaces below. Such illumination, I fancied, could not but flatter the countenance of every gentleman and lady fortunate enough to secure a table within these hallowed walls.

The walls were adorned with sporting prints and portraits of theatrical luminaries, their gilt frames catching the light as though determined to remind one of the illustrious personages who had supped here in years past. Between these artworks hung plush crimson draperies that lent a theatrical warmth to the proceedings, as if one were dining upon the stage of Drury Lane rather than in St. James's.

Our table, situated near enough to the hearth to benefit from its gentle warmth yet sufficiently removed to avoid any uncomfortable excesses of heat, was dressed in linens of such pristine whiteness as would satisfy the most fastidious of housekeepers. The silver gleamed with a polish that spoke of hours of dedicated labor, each piece arranged with mathematical precision alongside porcelain of the finest quality. A small crystal vase at the center contained a modest arrangement of seasonal blooms, providing a delicate counterpoint to the masculine robustness that characterised the majority of the decor.

All about us, waiters in their formal black attire navigated the narrow passages between tables with a dexterity born of long practice. They moved with the quiet efficiency of stage hands, appearing precisely when required and vanishing just as discreetly once their immediate purpose had been fulfilled. One could not help but admire the choreography of their service, the manner in which they anticipated the desires of the patrons often before such wants had been consciously acknowledged.

The clientele themselves embodied the very essence of London society. At a table to our right sat a gentleman whose silk waistcoat and carefully arranged cravat marked him as a denizen of the diplomatic corps, deep in conversation with a companion whose military bearing was unmistakable despite his civilian dress. Nearby, a party of theatrical folk engaged in spirited discourse, their voices carrying just sufficiently to convey their enthusiasm without revealing the particulars of their exchange. A distinguished matron occupied a corner table, accompanied by a young lady whom I took to be her daughter or niece, both attired in garments that, while fashionable, displayed that restraint which distinguishes true elegance from mere ostentation.

The atmosphere was suffused with the mingled aromas of roasted game, rich sauces, and the subtle perfume of the ladies present. Each breath seemed to carry the very essence of English culinary tradition, promising pleasures that would not disappoint the most discerning of palates. From the kitchens came the muted sounds of industry, the occasional clatter of pans serving only to reassure one that each dish was being prepared with the attention it deserved.

I observed that the walls, in addition to their decorative

elements, were panelled in dark wood to a considerable height, creating an atmosphere of comfortable enclosure despite the room's substantial dimensions. This architectural choice lent to our conversation a sense of privacy that encouraged candour, the panels seeming to absorb any excessive sounds and return only the pleasant murmur of civilised discourse.

As our first course arrived upon plates edged with a simple yet elegant pattern in blue, I could not but reflect upon the peculiar alchemy by which certain establishments transcend their mere physical attributes to become institutions. Rules had achieved this transformation decades before my birth and appeared set to maintain its position for generations yet to come. There was a timelessness about the place that rendered the concerns of the world outside its doors curiously remote, as though one had stepped not merely into a restaurant but into a sanctuary dedicated to the preservation of a particular vision of Englishness—one defined by quality, tradition, and an unapologetic celebration of the pleasures of the table.

I sat across from Dixon, who, despite his recent ordeal in prison, looked remarkably composed, even content. Alice was beside me, glancing at Dixon with a mix of worry and admiration. She still couldn't quite shake the horror of what he'd been through.

Dixon leaned back, studying the elegant array of dishes before us, but there was a hint of mischief in his gaze. "Prison was a most unpleasant experience, I won't lie," he said, his voice tinged with irony. "But it has a way of focusing the mind."

Alice watched him, her brow creased. "That's not something I'd care to test firsthand," she said softly.

I barely heard her, my mind tangled with the thought that had haunted me since we left Newgate: whatever happened to the Mechanist and Lovelace's diary? I could almost picture him out there, scheming, reading her discoveries, her notes, holding in his hands the very key to her genius. The thought of him possessing something so powerful made my stomach churn.

"Dixon," I said, unable to keep the edge of anxiety out of my voice, "the Mechanist is still out there. He's got Lovelace's diary. Who knows what he could do with it?"

Dixon, unfazed, wiped his hands with a napkin and then reached into his coat pocket, producing an evening newspaper. "As a matter of fact, Paul," he said, unfolding the paper with deliberate calm, "that particular problem has resolved itself."

He laid the paper flat on the table, and Alice and I leaned forward to read. There, tucked in the corner of the page, was a brief report:

"An enigmatic Italian magician, known only as 'The Mechanist,' has been found dead in a fire at the Trinity Buoy Wharf chainhouse. Authorities have been unable to determine his true identity, but signs of an explosion suggest that his clandestine operations may have led to his demise."

The explosion! The one that woke me up at night!

I stared at the words, a chill running through me. "Dead?" I muttered, barely believing it. "But... that's a very unlikely coincidence, isn't it?"

Dixon's mouth quirked in that sly, knowing smile of his. "Not a coincidence, Paul. He was a skilled cryptographer, as it turns out."

My mind raced, piecing it together. "You're saying he cracked Lovelace's code?"

Dixon took a measured sip of his wine, his expression maddeningly calm. "Only the code in my copy, Paul. The diary I gave him was... slightly modified."

I blinked, hardly daring to believe it. "Your copy?"

"Yes," Dixon replied, setting his glass down with the faintest smile. "A false lead, embedded with... let's say, a few cryptographic surprises. I couldn't risk giving him access to Lovelace's genuine work, so I crafted something more... dangerous."

Alice's eyes widened. "So you meant for this to happen?"

Dixon shrugged, resuming his meal with an air of absolute nonchalance. "Not exactly. I simply provided him with a diary that had some, shall we say, explosive insights. He was quite the magician, but cryptography is a delicate art. One wrong calculation..."

He trailed off, leaving the implication hanging between us, his attention seemingly back on his dinner.

I glanced at Alice, who looked as stunned as I felt. We sat in silence for a moment, the warmth of the room feeling almost surreal against the cold realisation of what Dixon had orchestrated. The Mechanist had chased his prize, found himself in Dixon's trap, and paid the ultimate price.

Our ruminations were interrupted abruptly and irreverently by the arrival of Saeed, who rushed into the dining room late and, in violation of all laws of propriety, clutching a feline to his chest. He extended his arms and held up Archimedes for all of us to see. Archimedes was alive and well. Both Archimedes and, especially, Saeed looked genuinely happy.

"Eureka!" said Saeed.

Chapter 34
The Aftermath

A soft golden light filtered through the tall windows of the British Museum Reading Room, casting elongated shadows across the polished wooden desks and illuminating dust motes that danced in the quiet air. I had claimed my usual spot near the eastern alcove, where the acoustics somehow dampened the shuffling of papers and occasional whispers that punctuated the scholarly silence. Before me lay several books on electromagnetic theory, their pages dog-eared and annotated in my increasingly cramped handwriting.

Six months had passed since that fateful day at Trinity Buoy Wharf. Six months since the Mechanist had met his fiery end among the twisted remnants of his laboratory. Six months of quiet study, of rebuilding, of trying to make sense of the maelstrom that had swept through my life like one of Professor Shaw's meteorological phenomena—chaotic, unpredictable, yet somehow governed by laws I was only beginning to comprehend.

Dixon had recovered remarkably well from his imprisonment. His reputation, far from being tarnished by the scandal, had been bolstered by the dramatic revelation of his innocence. The phonograph recording had caused a sensation, not only exonerating him but establishing a precedent for the use of such technology in criminal investigations. Sir Edward Bradford had championed this innovation within Scotland Yard, and Dixon had found himself something of a celebrity in scientific circles. He bore this newfound fame with characteristic indifference, returning to his experiments and occasional consultations with the police as though nothing extraordinary had occurred.

Alice had surprised me most of all. Our journey to Scotland had forged a bond between us that transcended the tentative friendship we'd shared before. She continued her work at The Gun, but her quick mind and natural curiosity had led Dixon to suggest she might assist in cataloguing his extensive library of scientific texts. She had taken to the task with enthusiasm, revealing a natural aptitude for organisation and an unexpected passion for natural philosophy. The quiet hours we now spent together, discussing everything from Faraday's field theory to the latest developments in analytical engines, had become the highlight of my weeks.

Yet as I sat in the hushed cathedral of knowledge that was the Reading Room, my thoughts kept returning to the diary—Ada Lovelace's genuine diary, which Dixon had revealed was safely stored in a vault at the Bank of England. He had shown it to me only once since the Mechanist's demise, allowing me a brief glimpse into the extraordinary mind of a woman who had seen further into the future of computation than perhaps anyone of her time. The diagrams and equations that filled those pages were beyond my complete understanding, but their implications were clear enough: Ada had envisioned machines that could perform tasks far beyond mere calculation, machines that might one day mimic the very processes of human thought, influence that thought, and fuse with it.

I wondered what she would have made of the Mechanist's twisted applications of her ideas. For according to Dixon, the Mechanist had indeed discovered something in Bertini's research—a crude yet effective method of influencing human behaviour through a combination of electromagnetic fields and specific auditory stimuli. The performance at Alexandra Palace had been no mere theatrical spectacle but a calculated experiment, testing the limits of mass influence on an unsuspecting audience.

The implications were deeply troubling. If one man with limited resources could exert such control over a crowd, what might a government or military power achieve with greater means? The thought reminded me of General von Waldersee's involvement, a connection that remained frustratingly obscure.

Von Waldersee, that stoic Prussian militarist, had vanished shortly after the incident at Alexandra Palace. Rumours placed him back in Berlin, where some said he had presented a detailed report to the German General Staff on what he termed "non-conventional military applications of electromagnetic science". The thought of such technology in military hands sent a chill through me, despite the warmth of the reading room.

And what of Swami Saraswati, that charismatic figure who had blessed the Mechanist's performance with such apparent spiritual authority? Dixon had discovered, through his extensive network of informants, that the Swami had boarded a steamer bound for Bombay in the days following the Alexandra Palace debacle. His disappearance had left a wake of disconsolate devotees among London's aristocratic circles, ladies who had invested both emotion and considerable financial resources in his teachings.

Yet there was something about the Swami that continued to puzzle me. Unlike the General, whose motives seemed clearly aligned with military advantage, the Swami's objectives remained enigmatic. Had he been merely another pawn in the Mechanist's game, a useful front to lend credibility to the performance? Or had he been pursuing some agenda of his own, perhaps seeing in the Mechanist's technology a means to enhance his own spiritual influence?

I sighed, closing the book before me. These questions might never find their answers, lost as they were in the ashes of the Trinity Buoy Wharf fire. Perhaps it was better that way. Some knowledge, as Dixon had implied with his doctored diary, carried dangers too great to be widely shared.

The thought of the false diary brought a grim smile to my face. Dixon had never explicitly confirmed that he had engineered the Mechanist's demise, maintaining that the explosion was the result of "cryptographic misinterpretation". But I had seen the calculating look in his eyes when he discussed it, the subtle satisfaction of a chess master who had anticipated his opponent's moves and laid a trap accordingly.

The ethical implications of such an action troubled me. Had Dixon appointed himself judge and executioner? Or had he merely provided a tool, leaving the Mechanist's fate in his own hands? These were questions I found myself reluctant to explore too deeply, perhaps out of fear that I might find my own moral compass wavering in the face of such complexity.

My reverie was interrupted by the soft clearing of a throat. I looked up to find Alice standing at the edge of my desk, a leather portfolio clutched in her hands. Her presence in the Reading Room was unexpected but not unwelcome.

"Professor Dixon sent me," she whispered, sliding into the chair opposite mine. "He thought you might find these interesting."

She placed the portfolio on the desk, carefully opening it to reveal several sheets of technical diagrams—designs for what appeared to be a more sophisticated version of the miniature phonograph I had used to record the Mechanist.

"He's been working with the engineers at the Royal Institution," Alice explained, her voice hushed but animated. "They believe they can improve the recording quality significantly. Sir Edward has shown great interest in the potential applications."

I studied the diagrams, noting the clever modifications to the sound capture mechanism. "This could transform criminal investigation," I murmured. "Imagine being able to preserve witness testimony exactly as spoken, to record confessions that cannot later be disputed."

Alice nodded, her eyes bright with enthusiasm. "And not just for police work. Think of preserving the voices of great orators, capturing musical performances, or even..." she hesitated, a slight blush colouring her cheeks, "personal messages for loved ones far away."

"It's remarkable," I agreed, carefully turning the pages to examine the details of the mechanism. "Technology that preserves the ephemeral, that bridges time itself."

As we bent our heads over the diagrams, discussing the implications of this new technology, I felt a curious sense of optimism rising within me. For all the dangers that the Mechanist's work had revealed, for all the potential for misuse that such advances carried, there remained the possibility of profound good.

I recalled Professor Napier Shaw's words from that lecture so many months ago, his grand pronouncements about "scientific methods conquering chaos". Perhaps there was truth in his vision after all. Perhaps the same principles that the Mechanist had sought to exploit for control and domination could, in the right hands, serve to expand human knowledge and connection.

Later that evening, as Alice and I walked along the Embankment, watching the setting sun gild the waters of the Thames, I shared these thoughts with her.

"Do you think we're doomed to see every scientific advance turned to harmful purposes?" I asked, gazing out at the river. "Or is there reason to hope that good might prevail?"

Alice was quiet for a moment, considering. "I think," she

said finally, "that knowledge itself is neither good nor evil. It's like the river before us—powerful, capable of destruction, but also life-giving and necessary." She turned to me, her expression earnest in the fading light. "The direction it takes depends on the channels we build for it."

I nodded, finding unexpected wisdom in her words. "Then we must be vigilant in building those channels," I said. "People like Dixon, who understand both the potential and the dangers."

"And people like you, Paul," she added softly, her hand finding mine in the gathering dusk. "Those who question, who seek understanding not for power but for truth."

Her touch was warm, grounding, a connection to something real and tangible amid the abstract concerns that had occupied my thoughts. In that moment, standing beside the ancient river that had witnessed the rise and fall of empires, the birth of countless innovations both benevolent and terrible, I felt a curious peace settle over me.

The Mechanist was gone, but the questions his existence had raised remained. The forces he had sought to harness—electromagnetic waves, human psychology, the power of suggestion—were still there to be explored, understood, and directed. In the coming years, I knew, the world would see technological advances beyond anything we could currently imagine. Some would bring destruction, others liberation. The difference would lie in the hands that guided them, in the intentions that shaped their application.

As the first stars appeared in the darkening sky, I made a silent promise to myself. I would continue my scientific studies, of course, pursuing the truth with all the rigour Dixon had instilled in me. But I would also remember the human element in all our equations, the ethical dimensions that no formula could fully capture. I would strive to be one of those who built channels for knowledge to flow toward healing rather than harm, toward connection rather than control.

Alice squeezed my hand gently, as if sensing my resolution. Together, we turned and began walking back toward the city, its gas lamps and electric lights now twinkling in the darkness, beacons of human ingenuity guiding our way home. In that simple moment, despite all I had witnessed of humanity's capacity for darkness, I found myself filled with a quiet but profound hope for what the future might hold.

About Atmosphere Press

Founded in 2015, Atmosphere Press was built on the principles of Honesty, Transparency, Professionalism, Kindness, and Making Your Book Awesome. As an ethical and author-friendly hybrid press, we stay true to that founding mission today.

If you're a reader, enter our giveaway for a free book here:

SCAN TO ENTER
BOOK GIVEAWAY

If you're a writer, submit your manuscript for consideration here:

SCAN TO SUBMIT
MANUSCRIPT

And always feel free to visit Atmosphere Press and our authors online at atmospherepress.com. See you there soon!

About the Author

The archive of Professor **Paul Gordon James**—long thought lost—has now been unearthed and made available for the first time. Born in Bath, Somerset, on July 4, 1870, Prof. James pursued his education at Christ Church, Oxford, before continuing his postgraduate studies at the Royal College of Science in London under the guidance of Prof. Reginald Dixon.

The collection of his papers, chronicled in The Night's Cipher, provides remarkable insights into 19th-century history, the nature of consciousness, and artificial intelligence—along with shocking revelations that may finally expose the true identity of Jack the Ripper. Equally controversial are the records concerning Prof. Dixon, a man whose actions remain the subject of fierce debate.

A collective of scholars, recognizing the profound historical and philosophical implications of these writings, has taken it upon themselves to preserve and publish them. With the support of Atmosphere Press, Prof. James's long-hidden work is now available to the public, allowing readers to explore the mysteries he left behind and determine the truth for themselves.

www.ingramcontent.com/pod-product-compliance
Ingram Content Group UK Ltd.
Pitfield, Milton Keynes, MK11 3LW, UK
UKHW040819040126
466575UK00002B/41

9 798901 740231